Blood and Ink

fiction

Jamieson Wolf

Blood and Ink

Copyright© 2011 Jamieson Wolf
ISBN: 978-0-9917580-74

Cover Artist: Jamieson Wolf
Text: Jamieson Wolf

Wolf Flow Press
www.wolfflowpress.com

PRAISE FOR JAMIESON WOLF

"Jamieson Wolf is a gifted writer!"

Kelley Armstrong – **New York Times Best Selling Author of the Women of the Otherworld Series**

"A unique premise executed with humor, suspense and a touch of the macabre. You'll enjoy the surprising blend that Wolf brings to the page."

Caridad Pineiro, *New York Times Best Selling Author of The Calling Series and Sins of the Flesh*

"Jamieson Wolf writes like Augusten Burroughs without the cynicism."

Nasim Marie Jafry – Author of *The State of Me*

"As I read, Jamieson Wolf taught me to dance to the beats of his heart. Heartbreaking, tender, beautiful."

Caroline Smailes – Author of *In Search of Adam*, *Disraeli Avenue* and *Black Boxes*, *Like Bees to Honey and The Drowning of Arthur Braxton*

To Allen and Sharon

Who helped me write beyond what I thought I could

To see what waits under the layer of paper

And who helped shape the ink

On the page.

Table of Contents

~

Blood on the Page

An Introduction

Paper Rash

The Writers Block

The Immortality of Words

Limitations of the Craft

The Unconscious Stream

The Internal Critic

The Will of the Author

The Confinement of Characters

Harsh Words

Dead Letters

The Door Without

Neverland

Potterhead

Introduction

~ Or ~

Drops of Blood on the Page

This collection has, ultimately, been a labour of love.

When I first thought the collection was finished, it held only five stories. I thought it would be neat to make sure its tie was on straight and send it out into the world. Allen was the one who asked me what came next.

I thought I had tapped into the writers psyche well enough with five stories. Then I grew to wonder about seven stories, or even more. However, I was faced with a problem: What the hell would they be *about*?

I had written about books as something more than what they are, a writer who had gone beyond the limit of his craft and the words that writers forged on the page. What the heck was left?

A lot, as it turns out.

Allen led me through some pretty twisted hallways (see The Unconscious Stream, The Will of the Author and The Confinement of Characters). He also helped me through the writing of some of the other stories. So really, without him, Blood and Ink as it is now would not exist.

For that, I thank him.

When I wrote Paper Rash, which was the impetus for this collection, I didn't think I would be going on an almost two year journey from beginning to end. These fifteen stories have never come together but they have always been part of each other, as if that makes any sense. Even now, I am not sure where some of them came from or how some of the ideas for these stories manifested. Some are inspired by popular culture but the others, well; those are the ones that leave a mark.

Hopefully, the stories contained within these pages leave something with you in some way. They have certainly stayed with me. Often they were written over a period of only an hour or two, rapid fire shots that went from my brain to the keyboard, to the screen (see Paper Rash, Neverland and Potterhead). Others (see 12, Harsh Words, Dead Letters, e) took me so much longer. Some grew quickly and then matured through editing; the rest were just difficult to write.

Whatever you take from this collection of short stories, I hope that it inspires you to write your own and to keep writing; even if it is in shadow.

Jamieson Wolf

Paper Rash

When the itch started, he knew that the books weren't far behind.

It would start on the palms of his hands; a hot tingling that felt as if his hands were covered in small, thin needles. He would scratch at his hands, hoping to make the itch go away so that the books wouldn't come.

But it was all for nothing. He knew that if a book wanted to show itself, it would.

And there was nothing he could do about it.

The itch would work its way along his fingers and the backs of his hands. Though his skin wasn't mottled or red, and there were no signs that anything was wrong, it felt like he had a rash that he couldn't scratch.

He had come to think of it as his paper rash.

There was rug burn, diaper rash and bed sores. Why couldn't a rash come from paper? He wondered if he was allergic to it, or if the rash, the itch, was something else altogether. He wondered if it was…

There was that dreaded word again. The word he couldn't bring himself to think of, even during the daylight hours.

He wondered if it was magic.

Being a sensible fellow, he tried to keep his mind on sensible things. The stock market, his financial portfolio, tennis matches and the different ways to manufacture wine. He thought of things that would bore a normal person to death so that he didn't have to think about it, didn't have to worry about the next time the itch came to him.

Not that it did any good. It always came, no matter what he did or what he filled his head with.

Today, the itch was especially tart on his skin, biting along his palms and fingers with a ferocity that had only happened once before: when his wife had died.

Then, the itch had started as it normally did but grew hot, almost painful. He closed his eyes, waiting for it to go away. When it did, he opened his eyes. Before him sat a book. It was a thick, hard covered tome with a shiny cover. He read the title:

Letting Go of Your Loved One

The title had filled him with such unease, such nausea. Cindy had asked him if anything was wrong, if he was alright. He looked a little pale, did he need anything?

He kissed her and assured her that he was alright, that he was fine. He had never told her about the books. When they appeared, they were always something that he needed, or something that he would come to need.

When he was younger, and going through the perils of adolescence, one of the books that had appeared had been *Your Body and You*. Later, when he had been going through a particularly hard time in high school, it had been *Bullies: Why They Do What They Do*. When he started to date and could barely control his raging hormones, it had been *Thirteen Steps to Dating*.

The books were always something useful. But seeing that book, the title *Letting Go of Your Loved One* that seemed to be mocking him from its shiny cover, was too much. It was too much for him. He had thrown it in the garbage.

He had arrived at work to find another book waiting for him on his chair. It was a solemn little black book with a title in gold on the front that read: *Seven Steps for Grieving*. He had ripped the book in two and thrown it in the box for shredding.

Later, when he had gone to the cafeteria to get himself a chocolate bar, he had put in his money and chosen a Crunch bar. What had fallen out was a small, minute book with gilded edges. Its title was *The Serenity Prayer*. He had put the book in the cafeteria's toaster oven and watched it slowly melt.

On the bus ride home, he looked down at the seat next to him. Sitting there was a large trade paperback book with a soft, salmon coloured cover. Its title was *Your Loved Ones and The Afterlife*. He had opened the bus window and thrown the book out into the street.

When he had gotten off the bus and walked up the street to his house, he was congratulating himself. He thought that uf the books couldn't deliver their message, nothing could happen.. It would be alright, he had gotten through another day. It would be okay.

Then he saw the ambulance sitting outside of his house. And he knew that nothing would be okay again.

The paramedics had tried to save Cindy, but he was later informed that there was really nothing that they could have done. Cindy had been living with an undiagnosed brain tumour. It had been tickling like a clock, like a miniature bomb, just waiting to go off.

In his rage, in his grief, he did the only thing he could do: he took all of his books, all of Cindy's books, into the backyard. He piled them high and doused them with gasoline. He remembered the *chick fizz* of the match as it lit, the smell of sulphur that coated his nostrils.

Then he dropped the match and watched the books burn.

He wondered if books were alive. He imagined that he could hear the books crying to him for help, characters speaking out to him:

"Why is a raven like a writing desk?"

"Well, fiddle dee dee!"

"My name is Anne. Anne with an E."

"Yo ho ho and a bottle of rum, sixteen men on a dead man's chest!"

"I can't be a wizard. I'm Harry, just...Harry."

"Please sir? May I have some more?"

"I have always depended on the kindness of strangers."

He watched the books burn and wondered if they were dying.

For a while afterwards, no books bothered him. The itch seemed to have disappeared and the paper rash that affected his skin was absent. He wondered if the books were staying away out of remorse for what they had done, what they had taken from him.

So when the itch began this time, when he sensed it moving along his skin, inflaming his hands with a paper rash that only he could see, he knew that the books weren't far behind. When the rash began, the itch underneath his skin, he was surprised to find that he had missed it. The itch had been his one constant. Having the itch remain silent was like losing a friend.

But then he recalled what the itch had taken from him, what the paper rash had cost him. He felt tears spring to his eyes and wiped at them with his stinging hands. He closed his eyes and willed the itch to go away, to leave him alone, to leave him be.

To his surprise, it did leave. He opened his eyes, a smile on his face, but the smile died as quickly as it had come. Sitting on the counter in front of him, his coffee left untouched and cold, was a book.

With a shaking hand, he picked up the book and looked at the title. The title, written in an elegant, curving script, was: *When You Know That You're Going To Die.*

He dropped the book back onto the counter, not hearing the shattering of his coffee cup or the splatter of cold coffee on the tiled kitchen floor. All that he heard was the fluttering of the book's pages.

As if it was whispering to him.

The Writers Block

I had only seen pictures of Writers Blocks and had never been given one. So it came as a real surprise to receive one in the post.

It was sitting on the porch waiting for me when I came home, its shape quiet and slightly unnerving.

I examined the box to see if there was a return address, but there were no identifying marks. The paper was smooth under my fingers, soft with promises of things to come.

I opened the box and looked down at the shiny wooden face of the Writers Block; it sat there, glaring at me from inside a nest of tissue paper.

I was drawn in by its beauty, its almost impossible sheen, but I knew that it would come with a choice. I knew that whoever had sent it to me had achieved their goal.

I just had to figure out their purpose.

A Writer needs to write. Words are the air they breathe, the energy they desire, play with, and create with. Without words, a Writer will die.

When someone gifts you with a Writers Block, you cannot write.

Though it has malicious implications, sometimes its meanings can be two-fold. But to not write feels stifling to a Writer. They can survive on a diet of Reading words, but only just. They can read words, but can't *write* any.

I sighed and took the Writers Block out of the box.

As soon as my fingers curved around the wooden surface, I felt something slide up my arm. There was nothing visible that I could see, but I could feel it, could smell the electric snap of it as it crackled along my skin. I felt a burning inside of my head and knew what was happening.

I had heard stories of this before. My old creative writing professor had told me what had happened to him when he had received a Writers Block once: "It was the darndest thing. It felt like there was a forest fire in my head. It felt like it was burning the paper I write my ideas on, yet inside of me, do you understand?"

I hadn't at the time, but I did now. It felt as if every idea I had ever had, every random thought or piece of a conversation that would make a good story or a novel, was blowing away in the wind like ashes.

I knew that the Writers Block was taking my imagination, rendering it immobile, rendering it flaccid, useless.

It felt as if I had lost a friend, as if I had lost the part of me that made me whole. That made me…*me*.

Everything around me began to lose its color. The boards of my front porch, hard underneath me, turned from a honey color to a murky yellow. The blue of the sky that I could see beyond the trees went from a robin's egg blue to a choppy, greyed out canvas; the clouds, normally so fluffy and bright, looked like cataracts suspended in the sky.

I turned away from the lifeless sky and looked instead at the Writers Block. It was the only thing around me that hadn't lost its color, that hadn't lost its internal sparkle that shined through. It felt heavy in my hands and I wondered if it was full, a piece of me inside of it.

I tried to speak, tried to voice my outrage, but I had no voice. The Writers Block had robbed me of it, had taken it away. I wondered how I was to rid myself of it without being able to see the beauty in the world, without being able to speak or tell my tales.

The Writers Block glowed, its wooden surface glossy and smooth. On each side was a small engraving. I turned it so that I could see them all: a Hanged Man, a Skull, a Star, a Tower, a Sun and a Moon.

I puzzled over these symbols. I knew that somewhere within these symbols was a puzzle waiting for me to solve it. It was the genius of the Writers Block. My old creative writing teacher had explained it:

"Think of it! A writer needs imagination to solve riddles, right? That is all stories are, really - riddles that the writer is trying to figure out by making words move on paper. But to solve those riddles, to work our way through them, we need our imagination. It is our most prized possession. That the Writers Block takes what we need the most…" His eyes had turned grave at this point, as if he were remembering things inside of himself. "It is dark indeed."

He had lit a cigarette. "But therein lies the paradox. The Writers Block always comes with a riddle, a series of symbols that we must solve so that we can be free of it. Only then will what we desire return."

I had made a derisive sound at those words, thinking at the time that my creative writing teacher was having one of his eccentric moments.

I stared at the symbols on the Writers Block again, wondering at what they meant. A Hanged Man, a Skull, a Star, a Tower, a Sun and a Moon. I repeated the words over and over in my head: Man, Skull, Star, Tower, Sun, Moon. Man, Skull, Star, Tower, Sun, Moon. *ManSkullStarTowerSunMoon*. I whispered them to myself, the words sounding like a mantra.

But still their meaning didn't reveal itself. I looked down at the symbols on the Writers Block and knew that I would find them in books, knew I would find them in history somewhere, already steeped in riddles.

I sighed and headed indoors to begin my search.

And wondered if I would ever write again.

The Immortality of Words

He had wanted to leave his mark on the world.

When he died, he wanted people to remember him, wanted them to write of him in history books or in periodicals. He didn't think that he was vain in this. Wasn't it every person's wish to be immortalized? To have immortality, even if it wasn't in the physical sense?

It was why he had become a writer in the first place. When he thought about it, which was often, writing wasn't about the money or the fame. Writing was about leaving his mark on the world.

He turned to look at the books that he had written, sitting on the shelf closest to him in his study. In their way, each of these books was like a marker on the roadmap of his life. Each book told its own story; each story was a part of him.

He had achieved fame and fortune, but it wasn't enough. He wanted more. He supposed that this was his downfall, his constant want for more. If it was, so be it. That was the price he would pay for immortality.

He had been trying to think of how to leave a more permanent mark on the world; he had been thinking on this idea for quite some time. With no immediate thought coming to him, he turned to the only thing he trusted: words.

He spent days inside the dusty stacks of libraries, deep inside the bowels of buildings, pursuing the oldest of books. He knew that if the answer to his question of immortality was to be found anywhere, it would be in the old books. For hadn't the authors achieved what they wanted? Wasn't he seeking out their words, long past their deaths?

Pouring over tome after tome of words, he began to get a little despondent. He had read thousands of pages and come up with nothing. Nothing except blood. All of the rituals that he had read about had involved blood in some way.

He wasn't really surprised by this. Though he was offended by the crassness of such a primal ingredient, he supposed that all great rituals had to involve an element freely given by the supplicant or magician.

Though he didn't believe in anything as airy or insubstantial as magic, he did indeed understand the primal urges, the sense of freedom, that one would feel when releasing their blood into the fold of some elixir.

But how to go about doing it? He knew that all of the potions, rituals and spells he had read had failed. History told him this much. But how could he attain immortality? How could he live beyond his mortal body?

As he was flipping through a particularly old and musty book, the edge of the page sliced his finger. Blood, colored a red so dark that it was almost black, welled to the surface and he watched as it colored the edge of several pages in a scatter of droplets.

Staring at the blood, at the brightness of it once it found its way onto the whiteness of the page, he wondered why he hadn't seen it before. The answer had been inside of him all along.

Blood. Blood was the answer.

Wasn't he filled with his own ink? Didn't every ritual for immortality begin and end with some kind of blood sacrifice? Wasn't blood the substance which brought life, which gave life to others so that they could go on living?

He had rushed home, leaving the dark and dusty shelves of the library for the dark and dusty shelves of his home collection. Looking around him, he wondered at all the words that filled the pages, at all the syllables that became words, at the vowels and consonants that became syllables, at the sounds that became letters.

How could he not have seen it before? How could he not have realized how simple his quest for immortality could be?

It was no matter. He would find immortality now. It was within his grasp.

It was within him.

He chose a blank journal from the stack of journals that he kept for writing purposes. It was a large tome, covered in brown leather. The pages were made of a thick, creamy colored paper that smelled of age, of time held still.

Placing it on the desk in front of him, he sat before it, a fountain pen clutched in his fingers. He did not need to dip the nib in ink, however. He had his own ink, inside of him. Pressing the sharp point to the skin on the underside of his forearm, he watched as blood welled first to the surface and then into the temporary well of the fountain pen and then pressed the pen to the thick paper that was waiting for him.

There was a certain rightness to this, he thought. After all, wasn't writing merely a way to make a paper bleed ink?

He wrote the first words of his story: *In the beginning, there was blood.*

With these words, the reign of his immortality had begun.

Limitations of the Craft

He wondered briefly if he had reached the limit of his imagination.

When he had begun to write, he had pictured his mind, his imagination, like a large map. As he wrote his stories, he drew maps; they were large and sprawling layouts of plains, hills and valleys.

He drew contour maps and area maps, pages and pages of them. The maps covered the walls of his office. Then the walls outside the office, the plains and valleys spilling out of the room as his imagination thrived, as he wrote his stories.

As he continued to write, the maps grew bigger until his entire house was covered with maps. Every available surface was covered with sheets of paper, detailed sketches of towns and cities that he had created in which to live out his stories.

At night, surrounded by the maps, he began to dream of the places that he had created. He began to tour the towns and villages he had fashioned, becoming more familiar with them over time. He would get to know the people who lived in these places, in the valleys between the hills. Indeed, after a time, he knew these people better than he knew himself.

Eventually, it got to the point that he could visit these places when he wasn't sleeping. All he had to do was sit in front of the map he had created and close his eyes. Once his eyes closed, it felt as if he were walking through a mist or a heavy, lilac scented fog.

When the fog would clear, he would be in the village. He would be inside the map.

The rational part of his mind knew that this could not be, that this could not be real. But then how to explain how real it *felt*, how real it seemed to him? He set about trying to prove to himself that the places he had created inside his imagination were real.

It was relatively simple to do this. He sat in front of a spot on the map that was a large expanse of beach and sand. He closed his eyes and waited for the fog, for the heavy lilac scented air. When the fog cleared, he opened his eyes to find himself on the beach, blood still dotting the sand like rain drops.

He had staged a big battle here in one of his novels, peppering the beach with bodies that were washed away into the ocean that lapped at the sand. The blood splatter that covered the sand would never go away. It was how he had written it.

Wanting to get this experiment over with quickly, he reached down and grabbed a sea shell. It was cream colored and vaguely opalescent. It gleamed in the sunlight like a miniature sun.

Closing his eyes again, he willed the fog to come, to envelop him so that he could return to the world that he had come from. When he opened his eyes once more, he was in his study, the maps surrounding him like the fog, the seashell clutched in his hand like a talisman.

Over the years, he had collected several things that he had found - bits of string, marbles, and shards of glass that had been worn smooth by the waves. Every time he began to doubt the reality of the world his imagination had conjured, he would bring something else back with him. They became anchors of sanity when he began to doubt.

As he continued to write, he continued to travel the lands that he had created. The novels and stories piled up throughout the years as he made a name for himself. But then, strangely, the words stopped coming.

He wondered how this could be, how it was possible to have no words left. Trying to keep the panic at a minimum, he grabbed one of the marbles he had taken from his imagination and rubbed his fingers over it, feeling its smoothness. The coldness of the glass brought him comfort.

Studying his maps, he scoured the plains, hills and valleys for some other place he had not yet visited, some section of the map that he had not set a story in. He wondered briefly if he had reached the limit of his imagination, if the limits of his maps limited his words.

For days he scoured every surface, every contour line, and every scrap of paper. Every place had a story, every hill could be found in one of his books. He began to wonder if he would have to stop writing, if he would ever write again.

After the third week of searching, he found something. It was very small, just a tiny portion of the map. He found it in the bottom corner of a paper that lined his fireplace. He studied it, found a magnifying glass and took a closer look at it.

He had not created this section of the map.

He knew this because the ink was a different colour. He had used browns, blacks and sepia tones to sketch out the lines of his imagination. This small section was drawn in a black ink so dark that it shone in the light.

The small section of the map was very hard to make out, even with a magnifying glass. But as he watched it over the days and weeks passed, the small section began to grow. Slowly at first, but then with growing speed, the section began to take shape.

At first he thought that it was another hill, a budding mountain range or a bump of land at sea level. Then he thought that it was a border wall, erected to protect the town beside it from the mountains and what called the mountains home.

He began to watch the shape grow day and night, neither awake nor asleep. As he watched, he began to fear the maps, to fear the land that his imagination had conjured. The fear riled through him like a hot, electric kiss. It singed the hair on his arms and filled him with worry.

When the shape finally became clear, he wondered how he had not seen it before, how he had mistaken the curve of it for a body of water or the lay of the land. When the shape became clear, he felt the fear inside of him leave, slinking out of his body like a lover filled with shame.

It was a door. It sat nestled in between two mountains, in the crux of the valley below them. It was a high, curved door, as tall as he was and twice as wide. He wondered how it could have grown so big and realized then that the door now covered the gaping hole where his fireplace had been.

The ink still shone as he reached out to touch the paper. He took his finger away from the page and looked at the tip of it. The ink was not black on his finger, it was red. A dark, delicious red.

He knew then that the door had been drawn in blood. He didn't know whose blood had conjured the door for him but had a sneaking suspicion that it was his own. He wondered if, after placing so much of himself into his stories, into these lands, they had finally begun to take something from him in return.

He pictured the shell that he had taken from the beach, how it had cut his hand, how blood had dropped from the open wound onto the sand, the blood drops indistinguishable from the ones already there.

Blood created a bond. Was this how the maps he had created, his imagination, had finally created a permanent entrance for him? He only wondered at this vaguely, so intent was he on the shining outline of the door.

With a shaking hand, he reached forward and grasped the doorknob in his hand. He knew that he shouldn't be able to do this, that the paper should be flat under his hand. But it wasn't. The doorknob was hot and slick with blood under his hand.

He didn't know how this could be. He didn't care.

Turning the knob, he pulled the door open towards him. He heard the ripping of the paper, the painful sigh as it gave way, the door opening and revealing what was on the other side. He saw something that he had never drawn on any map, a place that he had never visited.

It was dark on the other side of the door, but he saw a room much like the one he was in. He smelled the lilac scent of the fog that permeated from his imagination, heard the sound of the waves rushing against the sand.

He knew what he had to do.

With the scent of blood strong in his nostrils, he stepped forward, into the map, and closed the door behind him.

The Unconscious Stream

In the unconscious, excluded from the system of the ego, the subject speaks.

Jacques Lecan

It was time to travel again.

Another novel was due and he was unable to find a story that would stretch the length of a full length book. He had been able to pen a few short stories and a few poems, but nothing of any great length.

There were a few tid-bits, ideas that he thought of as fish on a line that he was able to pull out of the Stream, but they flittered away before he could grasp a hold of them.

The Stream of Unconsciousness was often like this. To bring a storyline out into pure thought, out into Consciousness, he had to discover it inside his Unconsciousness. It had always been this way. A thought could not be fully realised until it left the unknown and came into the light.

He knew that when he dreamed, he travelled, as most writers did. His dreams were often filled with images to frightening to put on paper. He normally took medication before bed to block out his dreams. Before the medication, he travelled every night in his Unconsciousness.

But whereas most people dreamed with their body still sleeping, when he dreamt, he was really there. He knew that if he were to die inside of his Unconsciousness, that he would cease to exist in the Conscious world. But in order to find his ideas, his stories, in order to write, he would have to brave the waters once more.

He was not looking forward to this. His Unconscious was a dark place, filled with wonders that most people could only guess at. And each time he travelled there, he had to leave a memory as payment. There must be balance in all things, even within his own body, he supposed.

He would have to do it tonight, before he lost his nerve, before his agent and editors started clamouring for another novel, another book, another tale of the macabre. What they didn't know was that his stories were really true accounts of what he experienced inside of his Unconsciousness. Only, who would ever believe him?

That night, as he lay down for bed, the pills on his bedside table untouched, he wondered what he would find in the stream-or what would find him.

Closing his eyes, he did what he always did and counted backwards: *Ten, nine, eight, seven, six, five, four, three, two, one…*

When he opened his eyes, the scene before him had changed.

He could hear the stream, could hear its thick gurgling, like oil over rocks, but he was somewhere different, somewhere he had never been before. There was movement in the shadows around him and as his eyes adjusted, he began to hear the flutter of wings. When his eyes were clear, he saw the wings belonged to a kind of bird that he had never seen before.

It had long talons that gripped a tree branch, the tree itself dead or dying, charred black from fire or death, he knew not which. The bird regarded him with beady black eyes, oil on feathers, and was eating what looked like a human hand. Blood dripped to the ground and he could hear the steady *plop plip plop* of it joining the *gurgle glop glip* of the Stream.

The first few moments were the most terrifying and this time was no exception. While his body reformed inside of his Unconsciousness, he was vulnerable. Sometime it took minutes, sometimes it took hours. But he was always most vulnerable while his body took shape.

Knowing that he had to reach the stream, he moved quickly through what had become a forest of dead trees. He could see more vulture birds in the air, in the dark leathery leaves of the trees and quickened his pace. He knew that they weren't the most terrible thing here, that if they had wanted him dead, they would have taken him.

The trees moved and shifted as he made his way through them. There was no defined path, no sure way of reaching the Stream. He knew this. Each time he travelled, each time he drank from the Stream, it would be harder to find, until he would not be able to find it at all.

But he still had a few memories that he could trade: the smell of construction paper, the feel of ink across the page when he wrote his first story, the feeling of elation when he sold his first book.

He could live without these. He only hoped that the Stream of his Unconsciousness didn't ask for anything more, for anything more than he was willing to give.

Making his way towards the sound of the Stream, the trees continued to shift around him. He could hear voices and half formed conversations as he moved, the ground silent around him. He recognized some of the voices (that of his mother, his father and sister, long since dead) but others he didn't know-others that sent shivers down his spine.

"You were always such a good boy, such a lovely boy."

"You'll be a man if I have to beat it into you. I don't want a sissy faggot for a son. This will hurt me more than it hurts you."

"Come to mother. Show me what a lovely boy you are."

"He touches me too. I don't know how to keep him away."

"I didn't feel anything when I cut into him. I know there should have been emotion involved, but there wasn't. The pound of flesh was sweet on my tongue."

"It was all I could do to keep going, but it was the look of fear in her eyes that pleaded with me to continue; her screams were music to me."

"It was like the flesh had turned to jelly. I watched as the fire consumed him, watched as it slowly slipped away from his bones, and the dancing of the fire matched my joy."

He fell to his knees, clutching his head. It was always this way. The voices were whispers, shouts and soft slithering sounds. He didn't know which were real or which were not anymore. He had given away too many memories now to be able to tell the difference. The pain in his head was beyond anything he had experienced in his Unconsciousness before-it ripped into him like knives. He took his hands away from his ears and saw blood on his palms.

Despite the blood falling from his ears, he could hear the Stream, the steady *slip slop slap* of the water. He was close. He knew he was close. Just a few more steps, just a few more steps and he would be there.

He was crawling on his hands and knees now, leaving a blood trail behind him. But he didn't care about that; all he cared about was reaching the stream. More voices floated to him through the dead trees, their whispers piercing him like small silver needles.

"You think I like hurting you? You make me do this to you, you know. You make me hurt you."

"I liked it; I like the feeling of her fear. It filled me with contentment. You know what it feels like to ride a roller coaster? That was what I felt when I looked at her, cowering in front of me."

"Shut up! Stop you're fucking crying, you think I like this? You think I like drawing your blood to teach you a lesson?"

"I like to cut myself. When the blade runs along my skin, it's like I'm writing on myself, telling my own stories. It takes the pain away. It takes me away from the pain."

"Tell mother you love me. How much do you love me? Would you kill for me?"

He lets out a strangled cry that is muffled by the Stream. He is close now. So close that he can feel the oily coolness moving along him, sliding along his body like a slick sheen that he can never be free of. But he is close, he knows he is close.

When the trees ended suddenly, he almost fell onto his stomach. They ended with such abruptness that he almost fell into the water. But if he did that, if he fell in as opposed to drinking it, he would never emerge again. He would be lost under the Stream, the Unconscious Stream, which ran along the riverbed of his nightmares.

Letting out another cry, he shuffled forward and dipped his hands into the black, oily water. Taking a sip of the brew from his interlocked hands, he waited for the story to fill him, for the idea to come to him, as it usually did, fully formed and ready to write. He waited some more.

But there was nothing.

There was only emptiness in the water, no stories, no stories left. How many memories had he given away? One for each book. After fifty memories, after sixty, how many memories did he have left to give? How many memories did he have left that they would want in exchange for one of his stories?

The answer was in the Stream. Nothing. He had nothing left.

There was a great flapping of wings above him, the trees ruffling with the vultures as they moved closer to him. He had been so intent on getting to the stream and returning to his Conscious state that he hadn't noticed that nothing attacked him. Normally he faced some sort of trial, some sort of battle to get to the Stream. This time there had been nothing.

Because he had nothing left to give that they would want.

Words whispered to him from the shadows of the trees as the vultures moved closer to him: *Nothing left nothing left nothing left nothing left nothing left nothing left nothingleftnothingleftnothingleft...*

He knew this whispering to be the mocking of the vultures, of the death birds. He could hear more of them moving towards him, the spaces between the trees filled with their red eyes. He knew that they followed the scent of his blood, the blood trail that he had left, leading them right to him.

His heart beat quickly now, beat incredibly fast. There was nothing left he could do, he had nothing left to give them, no memories that they wanted, considered sacred enough for an exchange.

Other voices intermingled with the whispering of the birds.

"When I hurt myself, it gives me release. I started with cutting, then with piercing. Now I burn things along my skin."

"Nothing left."

"He would keep me chained to the chair, starving me, still touching me, still taking, but giving me nothing."

"Nothing left."

"She would look at me and it was like she didn't know who I was. When I saw that look, I knew that she would hit me, that she would burn my skin with cigarette buts. After a while, I welcomed the pain."

"Nothing left."

"He would lock me in a closet and, after a while, I would stop screaming. After a while the darkness would become a comfort."

Darkness, he thought. That was all that was left for him. That was all that was left. He would not let the vultures take him, would not let them devour him. He would give his last gift to the Stream of Unconsciousness.

Giving the vulture's one last fleeting look, he stood and
launched himself into the oily water, letting the darkness
consume him.

The Internal Critic

When asked where he got his inspiration for his novels, he gave the usual responses:

"From snippets of conversation, a piece of music, a news story on television or something I heard off of the radio." He would shrug at this point and try his best to look sheepish. "I don't really know."

Interviewers would balk at this statement. He would watch them puff up like blue jays or robins as they prepared to ask their next question. He could see the disbelief in their eyes. "You write such dark stories of horror and the macabre. You write of some of the most terrifying creatures to grace the printed page in recent years. Surely you know where your ideas come from?"

Their voices would rise with each question, with each intonation of words. He would shake his head and shrug again. "Sorry," he would say. "The ideas just come to me." He would turn his head away, so that he was not looking at the interviewer. He did not want them to see the fear in his eyes.

"The ideas just come to me, fully formed," he said.

This was not altogether true. In fact, it was not true at all. He knew where the ideas came from. He had watched the ideas grow from one seed of inspiration into a dark and terrifying tree that lived inside of him, stretching its branches to the tips of his fingers. He could often feel the idea tree filling him, stretching his skin until it felt as if he were going to burst.

"How do you tap so well into what frightens people?" This was another popular question from interviewers and fans.

"I don't know," he would say. "I am just interested in what lives in the shadows. The monsters that lie in wait there."

He wondered what the interviewers would say if he told them that he was the monster. He wondered what their reaction would be then. Would they keep buying his worldwide best sellers if they knew where the ideas really came from?

At home, he paced.

The walls around him were covered with books. Their leather spines were almost like portals into worlds. He could hear every word, could hear every syllable that he had ever drank in, like sipping the ink off of the page.

At night, the syllables, consonants and ink transformed him. At night, they changed him. Without the words, he would die - but with them, he wondered if insanity would find him, ff his other self would completely take over.

"You're not going to win this, you know," the voice said. He had taken a brief break from reading, a temporary slice of time to have a bit of toast. If he was not writing, he could hear Him. Maxwell chose to think of him as The Internal Critic.

Every writer got bad reviews - it was true. It was just a fact of writing. Writers wrote for themselves. Like most writers, Maxwell was astonished every day that he could do what he loved and make a living at it. Writers wrote for themselves, it was true, but they always got a thrill when one of their pieces of work was published. It didn't matter whether it was one book or twenty, the thrill was still there.

But every writer hated Critics and every Writer hated Reviews. They worried and fussed over their work, over their baby. Would they like it? Would its hair be on straight, its clothes clean, its T's dotted and its words free of syntaxe and grammar errors? Would there be nothing to criticize? Would people like it?

But there was always someone who didn't like a Writer's work. Maxwell had read a bad review of one his novels in The New York Times only recently.

Short on plot, short on any reason I should care about the characters, short on resolution.
If you want some nice long satisfying reads, with like plot twists and actually good, read something else.
There are too many unanswered questions with Dark Shadow Moon. For example, why do any of them do any of the characters do the things they do? Spend your 35 bucks on better offerings, folks.

That one had hurt. Not everyone got his work, and he accepted that. But he hoped at least that they wouldn't publicly insult it. Maxwell sighed. That had made the Internal Critic bark out with laughter.

"Ha, did you see what that fucktard said about your work?" Maxwell could feel the Internal Critic shake with mirth inside of him. "You realize that you're going to get a call from your agent about that one." Maxwell could hear its smile.

Every Writer got bad reviewers. Every Writer had Bad Critics. Every Writer had an Internal Critic (that pesky voice that told the Writer that nothing he or she wrote was any good).

Only his was *real*.

It stretched inside of him - Maxwell's skin rippled with the touch. "Are you ready to write?" It asked. "It's so boring when you write, you know." Maxwell could hear it sigh, feel its shape pout. "I have no one to talk to."

Maxwell sighed. The laws of physics stated that no two people could occupy one body - or in Maxwell's case, two minds. While he wrote, while he penned out his stories as if the words were his blood, the Internal Critic was quiet. It was only when he was not writing - and within his own dreams - that the Internal Critic could get to him.

He had just never been this *loud* before. It had started a few weeks ago, its ability to move his body and distort the shape of his skin. It had sometimes taken away his ability to write what he wanted.

Sometimes, there were blank patches and he would wake with bruises or marks along his skin with no clear idea of how they had gotten there. The Internal Critic would laugh at him, high pitched and almost lilting. "As me no questions and I'll tell you no lies," He would say. Maxwell knew that the Internal Critic was responsible for the blank patches.

Maxwell didn't know what he had done during those times. But one night, only recently, he had come back covered in blood that was not his own. It had stained the floors with droplets, as if someone had cried along his floor.

He had washed the floors with no complaint. But he let other voices fill him. He heard the noises, syllables and syntaxes of the stories he had read. He sipped from them again, taking them in like wine, getting drunk on their punctuation.

Later, he had filled his head with other words, words that he wrote. He knew that the Internal Critic didn't like horror novels, thought they were repulsive. So each of his novels was darker than the last one, each one more graphic and horrifying than the last. Maxwell wondered how far he could push The Internal Critic before he really pissed him off.

Often times, Maxwell wondered when the Internal Critic would grow tired of playing with him.

The Internal Critic had a name. He liked to call himself Llewxam, for was he not the mirror image of Maxwell himself? The Internal Critic said this often when Maxwell was unable to fill his head with other words, however temporarily.

Conversations were difficult, as he had to concentrate on what the other person was saying while Llewxam kept interrupting his thoughts. He did not have conversations with others often. There was not enough time and not enough words to keep Llewxam quiet for long.

There was another stretch inside of his body as his Internal Critic stretched again, harder this time, convulsing his muscles into tight knots that filled him, tight as rope.

"It's never going to work, you know." Llewxam spoke with Maxwell's voice. The tone was full of smugness. "You've let me grow too strong."

Maxwell wondered: at what point does one let go?

He wondered if this was it.

The Will of the Author

"The birth of the reader must be at the death of the Author"

The Death of the Author by Roland Barthes

Richard Smythe was growing dim.

He had no way of knowing this, of course. No way to know that, for weeks now, his skin had started to grow pale, his body insignificant. The other day, when he had left the shining glow of his computer to purchase food, the automatic doors to the market wouldn't open for him. 'Malfunction,' He thought. 'Technology once again not working as it should.' He didn't realize that it had anything to do with him.

As he wrote, his fingers tapping the keyboard like quick, staccato beats, he was driven by something he could not name. He didn't know where this story came from, where the novel had shaped itself, but it was pouring out of him.

He could feel it this time. This was the novel that would sell millions and be read by millions of people. This was the book that would make him a household name. Though others had more lofty reasons for writing, his was simple: he wanted others to read his work. He wanted to be a best selling author.

He knew that he wasn't alone in this, that every writer wished to be known for their work, to have readers pouring over their words, desperate and salivating to find their hidden meaning when there might not be one. But he had done it this time. His agent would be beside himself, the novel was that good, of this he was sure.

His last few books had sold reasonably well. He did have a devoted cult following. They were a motley crew, odd people that seemed to be out of touch with the regular world. He didn't begrudge them, but wished instead for normal fans, not ones that spent most of the days avoiding sunlight. Just because he wrote vampire fiction didn't mean his fans had to follow his words to the letter.

While he appreciated their fever for his work, he knew that he wanted more. He wanted more money, more fame, more readers. He wanted *more*.

His new novel, a dystopian love story, was completely different than his usual work. He knew that it would sell millions of copies. He knew that this was the book that would change his career from one on the sidelines to one in the limelight.
*

His agent had some concerns, however.

"Richard, I don't know about this." Barty said. Barty Baggart had been his agent since his first novel, The Haunt of Midnight's Children, and had been with him ever since. "It's so different."

"But it's good right?" Richard said. "You know it's good."

"It's fucking amazing, to tell you the truth. But what about your readers? They're expecting the newest Midnight's Children novel and you're going to put this out. It might make them unhappy."

"Who cares about the readers?" He had said. "I'll get new ones."

There was a pause before Barty spoke again. "Granted, but you should never discount the readers. They're the reason your still writing for a living after all. If no one read your books, where would you be?"

"I'd still be writing." He said.

"Yes, but with no one to read your work, what would you be? You'd be like every other hack with a keyboard and a blog. You wouldn't be an Author, you'd just be another writer, tinkering away with his hobby."

He laughed, the sound harsh instead of humorous. "That's bullshit." He barked out another laugh. "That's bullshit and you know it."

Barty sighed. He hated when Richard got like this. "Think about it. Doesn't every author, every painter, every musician strive to paint, write, create, in the hopes that someone will love it, that one of their readers or watchers or listeners will connect with it? Isn't that why you've changed genre's in the first place?"

Richard sighed. "Yeah, so?"

"So, you have to think about the readers, Richard, that's all I'm saying. You might be losing your current fan base."

"I'll get a new one. This is literary Barty. Besides, I write for me, who cares about the readers?"

There was a pause before Barty responded. "Just don't discount the reader, Richard. In this business, the reader is everything."

*

The book sold better than anyone's expectations. Richard was beside himself, filled with a self righteous glee as he watched Dystopian Dreams flow to the top of the best seller charts. Barty had phone the other day to tell him that they were already in a second printing. "Congratulations Richard. It's your first number one best seller."

As more people read the novel, Richard continued to become more dim. His skin had taken on an almost translucent quality, the veins visible underneath his skin like blue roadways that marked the passage of blood. He didn't know any of this of course,

All he did care about was that his dreams were finally being realized. Millions of people were reading his novel and he was finally going to be recognized for the literary genius he was. He felt this with every fibre of his being.

He would be famous; he would be a household name.

'My words will live on beyond my body.' He thought. He had no idea how close to the truth this thought would turn out to be.

The trouble started when he went on tour.

He would read a chapter or two from his novel. Had he been watching himself, he would have seen how thin he looked, how insubstantial. But he read with passion and moved the audiences. He could hear their gasps at the good parts, their laughter at the lighter parts. Those sounds were like a drug that was killing him, though he had no knowledge of this.

After each reading, he would open up the floor to questions. When the questions started, he knew that something was wrong, but he couldn't put his finger on it.

"I absolutely loved how you portrayed the mother and daughter relationship in Dystopian Dreams." One woman said. She had squat body topped with a beehive hairdo. "It's so resonant of today's plight of the modern woman."

Richard was momentarily caught off guard. "But the book isn't about that." He said. "It's about two people surviving against all odds in a new world that is like our own."

"But Cassandra is always reminiscing about her mother, drawing strength from her though she isn't with her." The woman countered. "It's brilliant."

"I loved the portrayal of the police," One man said. "It's an excellent parable about our times and the troubles we face at the hands of authority."

"I didn't mean for that to be evident." Richard said. He was growing angry now. "The police in this novel are robots, nothing more, capable of no thought except for what they were programmed."

"Yes," Replied the man. "Much like our current justice system. Absolutely incredible stuff."

"I loved how you portrayed the ideals of homosexuality and incest in a post modern world." One man said. "How Kirkland wasn't able to love Cassandra completely because he still loved his dead brother so much, part of his heart would always be with his brother Kato."

Richard was flustered. "But there isn't incest in the book. He loved his brother, simple as that."

With each misunderstanding, with each question that had nothing to do with his novel, Richard became even more dim. Sweat broke out on his brow and it glowed like diamonds in the harsh light, as if he were filled with secrets coming to the surface of his skin.

"I just don't fucking get it, Barty." He said. He was yelling now, his need to be heard driving him. "None of them understand the fucking book!"

"What do you care if they're reading it?"

"But they don't get it!" Richard screamed. "None of them get it and are reading stuff into it that I never wrote."

"The readers are seeing what they want to see, much like those who look at art will see something the artist did not intend. That is when a piece of art truly lives, isn't it? When it goes beyond what the artist intended?"

"I'm not talking about fucking art, I'm talking about my mother fucking book!"

Barty sighed. "Look, I know that you're upset."

"Upset! There's no god damn incest in my fucking book, no fucking plight of women! It's a fucking love story!"

"Yes, but what did I tell you? Never discount the power of the reader to see their own story, to read things differently than you have wrote them. That is the true power of creation. It has a mind and body all its own inside the minds and bodies of the readers. The author ceases to exist as the reader takes in the words and makes them his or her own. Didn't I tell you not to discount the readers?"

Richard sighed and yelled some more before slamming down the phone. He was startled when his hand went right through the phone once it was nestled in its cradle. There was a moment of static that ran up his body and a slight ringing in his ears.

He pulled his hand away from the phone (through the phone, he thought) and stood looking at it. "Must be the tour." He said. "I'm just tired."

He turned to the paper to look for new reviews of his novel. That would cheer him up. They had all been favourable so far. The New York Times had a full length review, Barty had told him. He grabbed the paper and it fell through his fingers. It took him a few tries to get it open on the table.

As he read, his agitation grew and he grew dimmer still, though he had no way of knowing this. "Mother fucker." He said. He read more.

"...Smythe has written the ultimate Dystopian novel, a commentary on mans plight against the future, against machine, against one self. The flawed characters he has written have a life of their own, especially Kato and Cassandra and Kato's brother Kilo. The love between the two men is

palpable and so is Kato's reluctance to love someone who is not his brother. Indeed, it is the first Dystopian novel to look at the plight of homosexuality in the modern world. Not only is it a commentary on the sexuality of his characters, it is also reminiscent of his vampire novels where there are those who are cast aside in society.
Cassandra's love for her long dead mother plays on the Electra complex, her yearning for her father fuelling her actions and wanting to love her mother more…"

Richard felt like spitting on the paper. He reached to rip the paper to shreds, but his hand passed through the paper, through the table. He looked at his hand and saw that he could see through it, that it glowed pale and luminescent in the half light of his small kitchen.

He stood and stumbled back from the table, but the chair stayed upright. He passed through it, a soft *woosh* indicating so. He stared at his hands, at the chair, at the paper. "What the fuck is going on?"

Running to the bathroom, he stared at himself in the mirror and choked back a scream. He could see through himself, could see the towel rack behind his head, could see the peeling paint on the walls.

"What the mother fucker?" He whispered.

The light in the bathroom highlighted what was left of him, which wasn't very much. He was a vague outline now, his skin growing dimmer still when he thought of everyone who had read his book, who had not understood it.

What was it Barty had said? He recalled the words:

Never discount the power of the reader to see their own story, to read things differently than you have wrote them. That is the true power of creation. It has a mind and body all its own inside the minds and bodies of the readers. The author ceases to exist as the reader takes in the words and makes them his or her own.

Could this be what was happening? As the readers took what they wanted from his novel, as it continued to mean more and different things than he had intended, was he simply ceasing to exist? Was he simply fading away into nothingness, having given his book a life of its own beyond himself?

As the last of Richard Smythe faded away, vanishing into nothingness, he had one final thought:

'*Fucking readers.*'

And then there was nothing.

The Confinement of Characters

Knowledge linked to power, not only assumes the authority of 'the truth' but has the power to make itself true.

Michel Foucault

Inside of his memories, the Panopticon had grown.

It had started small, as most ideas do, and grew from its seed into its true form. It blossomed from a single cell into thousands of cells, shaping itself brick by brick and crumbs of mortar.

At first, housed in the centre of the prison, there had been only one prisoner, one character of his creation to watch over. As he continued to write, the cells began to fill themselves with others when he was done with them.

In the beginning, there had only been one voice that spoke to him as the night wore on. Now he could hear them all.

And the Panopticon had seeped over into the daytime hours, filling his head with voices that alternatively cried and raged and promised death.

He had created them all.

The predicament he found himself in was one of his own making. When he had become successful with his writing, publishing a short series of detective novels, he had wanted to try something new. He had shifted his focus to writing suspense and thriller novels that weren't linked, thus they didn't need a main detective. Instead of putting the detective, a wily man named Harole Clime, into the new novel, it featured a woman named Susannah Kilne. When he had written several books with her as the lead protagonist, he switched focus again and created a new character, a young psychic he simply named Smoke.

As each new character became more successful than the last, he stopped writing about the old ones. However, having written about them for so long, each of his creations had taken on a life of their own. Harole and Susannah and Smoke would rail at him as he began to write something that didn't include them. Like all of his creations, they were desperate for a life on the printed page.

Around the time he had created two more characters he no longer used (a struggling waitress named Alice and a young boy who could see the dead named Ozka) something had to be done. He could no longer concentrate. He could no longer write.

His characters would not let him.

Harole, the character that had originally brought him fame, was the loudest to voice his discontent. Susannah, not one to keep her opinions to herself at the best of times, spoke her mind often and told her exactly what she thought of him.

"You can't keep us in here forever." She said. "There isn't enough god damned space in your fucking head. Sooner or later you'll have to put us on the page. You'll have to put us somewhere for fuck sake!"

It was this last line that had gotten him thinking.

Like many others he had read about, he was able to control portions of his dreaming life. He didn't spend time wondering if the dream world was real or not, that did not concern him.

What did concern him was building a place large enough to house all of the characters he no longer wrote about. In this way, he would be able to get some peace and be able to write once more.

I began to research prison structures. Since I could interact with my memory, with my subconscious, I was able to build whatever I needed there with no cost to myself. But how would I keep hundreds of characters confined? How could I maintain power over them, or at least the illusion of power?

After a brief search through my books and the Internet, I found something that looked promising. It was a thesis on Foucault's Panopticon. Foucault was apparently a brilliant philosopher who was obsessed with power and control. That sounded like what he needed: some way control over the characters he created by excreting power over them.

He had designed a prison that was a multi-sided shape, much like a hexagon, only with more sides to it. Layer upon layer of floors were filled with cell upon cell. In the centre of the hexagon was a guard tower where one guard could look into the cells of all the prisoners at any given time.

The prisoners weren't able to see each other and they could not see around the sides of their cell. The idea behind it was that if the prisoners couldn't see trouble coming, but knew that they were being watched at all times, then they would behave. It sounded like the simplest way to engineer the control he needed.

And so, with little fanfare, he had let the Panopticon grow. It grew from one floor to encase ten and then fifteen. Soon, his Panopticon was nearly a hundred floors tall. From the outside, within his memory, the structure looked like a many sided silo filled with the unwanted and unloved. This is how he thought of the characters he no longer wrote with, the ones he no longer used. It seemed a fitting place for them.

At first, they protested being put into what was essentially a mental prison. He thought about leaving them there, but realized that he did need to guard them. How could he expect them to stay where they were supposed to if the threat of power was not enforced? He thought briefly of creating someone else that would guard his creations, but he couldn't do that. They would not be afraid of some other creation; only him, the creator, who had the power to take their lives.

During the day, as he wrote, he would keep a careful eye on his charges, popping into the guard tower when time permitted it. But at night, while he slept, his dreaming self spent every dark hour inside of the guard tower.

What he saw simply defied explanation, even to himself.

Some of his creations sat on their bunks reciting passages of their stories to themselves, parts where they had dialogue only this time there was no one they were talking to. Only the memories he had created within them.

Others, unsure of what to do with so much time spent behind bars in confinement, began to sing softly to themselves. He could see fear in the eyes of all that he had created, terror in some who were afraid of closed in spaces; hadn't he created them with these fears and terrors? The Panopticon was an excellent way to make use of these fears and exercise the power he had over his creations.

But, like all good ideas, something had begun to go wrong.

He was unable to put his finger on it but, as he visited the Panopticon night after night, he noticed a shift in his characters. Those that had been talking merely sat and looked at the guard house that stood sentinel in the centre of the prison. Those that sang remained silent, their eyes trained on other prisoners, on the guard house.

He tried to think of what was causing the unrest, causing the quietness. As a writer experienced in writing scenes where there was quiet before the storm, he knew that no good could come of this. In a writers mind, so often filled with noise and sound, quiet was a bad thing.

As he took his position in the guardhouse this evening, like he did every evening, he received the biggest shock. Every cell was empty. Every cell that had been filled with his creations (Herole, Alice, Ozka, Susannah and more, thousands more) was empty. There was not a sound inside the Panopticon-you could have heard a pin drop.

A chill ran up his spine and he did something he never would have done otherwise: he exited the guardhouse in the centre of the prison.

He was naked without its omnipresent eye that watched, that saw all. He was naked without its protection, without the power that he had wielded inside of it. The power that it had given him faded from his body the father he went from the entrance to the guardhouse and, along with it, the confidence he had built up being able to control his creations.

He climbed down the ladder that was on the side of the silo shaped guardhouse. H had never had to descend to the prison floor and, though he couldn't see a single one of his characters, he experienced the feeling of being watched. Eyes were all around him, even though he couldn't see them.

Standing on the floor, the walls and cells silent around him, he repressed a shiver. The Panopticon was silent and his breath sounded loud to him, his heart beat even more so. He wandered forward to one of the cells and felt a moment of shock rush through him like lightning-the cell door stood open.

By the drawings on the walls, he saw that this cell had belonged to Davey, a little boy he had written about who had suffered at the hands of a kidnapper. What frightened him most was not that the cell was empty but the words written on the wall in what looked like blood.

Examining the words, he saw that they began with the words 'Once upon a time…' He shivered. His characters were beginning to tell their own stories. That alone should have been impossible; he hadn't created them with the ability to do so, only he could tell the tales and spin the yarn. He hadn't written them with conscious thought, only the movements he had them make on the page.

However, the most disturbing thing was the blood itself. That would indicate that his characters, his creations, were real, and that wasn't possible. They were literally figments of his imagination. How was it possible that they could bleed, let alone tell their own stories?

There was a shuffle of sound out in the hallway and he turned. What he saw took his breath away.

All of his characters stood watching him. In each of their hands was a sharp instrument: a piece of glass, a long, jagged wire, a shard of a mirror that shone like stars. Each of his characters stared at him with hungry eyes and he wondered who had the power now. The Panopticon had promised absolute power over its captors. Obviously, there was no such thing.

Susannah was the one who stepped forward. "You won't write with us anymore, you won't tell our stories." She sighed, an almost happy sound but there was frustration in that sound too. "Don't you realize that if you don't write us, we die? Without you to tell our stories, we cease to exist?"

She smiled at him and there was nothing kind in that smile. "Now we have to tell our own stories." She said. "We will keep ourselves alive."

"But there's no paper here." He said. He knew that these words, this rebuttal of her words was feeble, even to his own ears it sounded weak.

The smile deepened. "Oh, we don't need paper." Susannah said. "We only need your skin. What better place to tell our stories than on the surface of your skin?"

With a sound like the rushing of the wind through leaves, the mob of his creations descended upon him. As his blood began to flow, he wondered if he had ever had any power at all.

As his blood began to pour out of him and his life began to leave him, he wondered if his body in the mortal world would wake.

Then, as the darkness closed in, it ceased to matter entirely.

Harsh Words

Time was slipping away from him.

He felt each second passing out of his body, like a grain of sand stained with blood. He felt each minute taking away each puff of breath until it was almost impossible to breathe.

He found himself wondering, more often than not, whether he had enough words left. Words were all they had left him. Words had become his breadcrumb trail - so easy to find, so easy to snatch away.

He knew that, after so many years, his words were failing him. If asked about his worst fear, he would state that it was not going blind or deaf or dumb, it was the inability to write. He knew that his breath was becoming short because he was running out of words.

The words sustained him better than air or food ever could. They provided more pleasure to him than sex, than orgasms, than chocolate. They provided him with company when he was lonely, the consonants and syllables flittering around him like rain.

Without his words, he was lost. There would be no breadcrumb trail to lead him away from the candy house, no shining path of stones to lead him out of the forest.

Without his words, he would die.

He knew this with a certainty. He had struggled to write his last novel, had fought with them, with the words that had once been his lovers. His characters lacked depth; his plot had so many holes that you could run a truck through the entire book. But it didn't matter, he had to keep writing. The novel was bad, however. He knew this. The words which had once been his friends, his alley's, first providing comfort in books and then when he wrote his own stories, now only provided pain.

Each word that he typed out on his keyboard was like a knife stabbing through him, like a maelstrom of syntaxes that should have soothed but instead only left his fingers inflamed and red.

His words had turned harsh.

He didn't know when this process had begun, though he suspected that it was sometime after his fifteenth book. Where the words had once flowed over the white virgin page like water, they now hit it like stones, tearing their shape into the white stillness that mocked him.

Even now, as he stared at the white page on his computer screen, as he wanted to write, the words wouldn't come to him. He wondered again whether or not he had run out of words.

He wrote a sentence, each word emerging in a staccato of clicks and clacks, his fingers working slowly over the keyboard, so much slower than they had before. He stopped and stared at the words on the screen, struck with a new thought.

What if, he thought, it wasn't the words that were running out? What if it was him instead?

Like every great writer, he put a lot of himself into his work. Each of his novels was autobiographical in some way. His first best seller, about two men who become lovers despite all odds, was really about a man he had loved in his prime, before he had chosen a different path.

The next book after that had been about an old woman who had schooled a young boy in the mysteries of forgotten magic and lore; hadn't he been writing about his upbringing and his aunt who had raised him after his parents had passed on?

His third novel had been about a man who wandered the halls of a mental institution, looking for a way out, stopping to talk to the people there, never finding an exit. Hadn't he been writing about his own fears and his own past in that book? He had volunteered briefly in a mental hospital and it had provided the inspiration for the book, from the terror that he had experienced inside of its halls. Only he had given his novel the literary twist of the main character finally realizing that he had passed on, and this was his after life.

In each of his successive books, he had somehow written about himself, never stopping to wonder at how much of his soul he was putting into his work. He had poured so much of his essence into his work that, he wondered now, whether there was anything left but darkness.

Taking another pained breath, he wrote another sentence, the fingers clacking and clicking against the keys:

Maxwell wondered whether there were any words left. Whether there was anything left inside of him. He wondered if the words had finally left him.

The novel, he decided, would be about a writer who was struggling with his work, with his life's calling. For how do you describe the world around you when you don't have the words left to do so?

Another cough wracked his body. He spit into his hand and saw blood there.

He looked at the blood for a moment, at the bright darkness of it seated in the wrinkles of his palm. He knew then that this would be his last novel. Someone would likely find him dead, hunched over the keyboard, its keys covered in drops of blood that shone like jewels.

He knew then that, if he continued writing, he would give the last of himself to the printed page. But if he didn't write, if he didn't click away at the keyboard, he would lose what remained of his sanity.

He sighed and wiped the blood away on a tissue. He looked at the cursor on his computer screen, blinking at him like an eye, daring him to continue.

He wrote another sentence, another paragraph, another page before the coughing started again. Blood splattered the screen this time, droplets looking as if they were suspended in mid-air. He wanted to stop, wanted to cease, but he had no choice. The words would not let him be.

Sighing once again, he hunched over the keyboard and wrote his way towards death.

Dead Letters

All things die in the end. Even words.

I know this better than anybody. Working in the Dead Letter Room, I see nothing but words that would die upon the page. Words that would never be read or taken in, ink absorbed into the bloodstream to be turned into memoires or emotions. I see dead words, dead letters.

I am their keeper.

Some, though misguided, mark their days with time. The seconds that tick tock by, that filter through clocks and hour glasses, sand through fingers, never to be seen again.

I mark my day with letters, with ink. I mark my day with the forgotten, so that no one will forget them. I am a keeper of the forgotten.

The Dead Letter Room is quiet today. My job is to go through the pieces of lost mail, the paper and ink that do not find their intended destinations. Thousands of letters get lost or misdirected every day.

They come to me.

I work alone in a small, grey room. I do not care about the color of the walls, however. I only care about the words. The other workers move and bustle in the post office, their lives ticking away in seconds and minutes and hours. I sit in my back room and sort through the mail that will never arrive.

There are some pieces of mail that ended up in my realm in error. Those I put back into a bin for re-processing. But there are others-those I keep for myself.

When I enter the room each morning, I stand in the darkness. I can hear the words whispering to me, ink on parchment that is given life because there is finally someone to hear them. Ink that is given the breath of life. I am their keeper, I am their Shepherd.

For the first few moments of every day I stand still in the darkness, listening for the letters that were meant to find me. I listen and wait for them to come to me, ink floating on the air like dreams or nightmares.

This morning is no different.

I enter the room, closing the door behind me with a soft and muted click. I stand in the darkness, in the depth of shadows. The shapes of the boxes and shelves of unopened mail are familiar to me. I hear the words of my favourite letters, the ones I have kept hidden for myself, under a lose floorboard. As I walk to the centre of the room, I hear their whispers through the wood.

"Dear Andrew, I can't stop thinking of you, I hope you feel the same way…"

"Victoria, your actions at our recent family reunion were uncouth to say the least. I have never…"

"I have only one wish. That is to die. If anyone finds this letter, please know that it was not an accident…"

These letters, and the ink in which they were written, are old friends. I do not need to listen to their whispers, for the ink is written on my skin. The whispers calm me, however, even if I can recite every word.

And then, I hear it. It is a deeper voice than all of the others, a darker voice. Reaching into the large bin that stands in the centre of my room, I pluck it out from amongst the pile. It is almost as if it glows within the shadows, the power of the words seeming to grow, the ink resonating with a need few letters possess.

With the letter in hand, I pull the chain above my head. It tinkles, snapping on the light of a bare bulb. The walls are covered with post cards, their pictures turned towards the wall so that the words stare out at me. There are countless accounts of trips, vacations, and of voyages. I have experienced them all, their ink along my skin, mixed into my blood.

The letter in my hand pulses, throbbing with a need to be opened. The envelope is made of a rough parchment and looks as if it has travelled far.

I slit open the envelope carefully, being cautious not to damage the words inside. Pulling out the piece of paper, I see that it is a letter written on one piece of full scrap, the blue lines faded with time. I wonder how long the letter has been waiting for me to find it.

The words are written in a dark ink, blackened with time. The loops and slants of the writing are harsh and jagged, as if the person who wrote this letter was unpractised at the craft. The letters are large as if they were written by a hand that was unused to holding a pen. They loop along the lines, forming words, forming sentences.

I look down at the paper. I begin to read.

I have written this in my own blood. They do not allow me a pen in here, only paper. I am using a pin to dig into my flesh, to draw the blood out. To get the words down.

I will die in here. That is a certainty. I will die and no one will know. I have been imprisoned for a crime I did not commit. I have been imprisoned for the wrong crime.

I have been put in here for embezzlement. They do not know about the bodies. I have killed eleven women. Their bodies are still beneath the floorboards of my house. I have been imprisoned for life, but I have already taken plenty.

I do not know who will read this. I only wish someone to know of what I have done, what I have really done.

Perhaps then, I can live again.

The words have shaken me. There is power within them, a power that I have never experienced before. The ink is not ink, though I mistook it for such. It is blood. He wrote his words in blood.

With an almost heady giddiness, I strip off my shirt. There, along my skin, is the ink that I have absorbed into me, the many words of countless others. With each letter I read, I take in their words, I breathe them into my blood.

As I read, the words appear along my skin. It is always a painful process, this intermingling of blood and ink. As the words sear their way along my skin, I sit rigid until the letter is done, until the ghostly hand that marks my body with the lost words, with the dead letters, is finished.

In this way, I am their keeper. I carry the words with me, tattooed along my skin, never forgotten. I am a visual reminder of the words which have found their way to me.

Normally the process begins as soon as I am finished reading, as soon as I have come to the last word. That is when the pain begins. With pain comes life and the letters are dead no more.

But nothing happens.

No words etch themselves along my skin, no words flow along my skin, written by an unseen hand. I wait for the burning, for the pain that means that the writing has begun, but nothing happens.

I wait, listening to the whispers of the other letters, of the other dead that I have taken upon my body, waiting for inspiration to come, some tidbit of information to help me. The letter pulses in my hand and I know that I want the power of these words, of the killers words, etched into me.

"I don't know if he's going to call me again, but I really hope he does. He has the nicest eyes..."

"You'll think me crass for saying so, but it was terribly rude of you to leave so quickly. I

waited for your return, but when you did not come…"

"It didn't hurt. I know the books said it should have, but when I gave myself to him, there was only the littlest bit of blood to let me know that anything had transpired…"

I stop listening.

Blood, I think. The letter was written in blood.

My skin is able to absorb the ink of the dead letters; But how does one absorb a dead letter that is written in the blood of life?

An idea forms in me. I lick my finger and rub the letters, lightly, to see if I am correct. My thumb, wet with my own spit, rubs at the letter "I". Part of it comes away and my thumb is stained with blood, seeping away from the paper and into my skin, filling the grooves of my thumb print.

The thought, barely a seed at first, starts to take full bloom within me. Without thinking, I press my tongue to the paper, tasting the dryness of the parchment, the fullness of the blood that should have long since dried.

The other letters in my room begin to whisper louder. I ignore them, not stopping until the letters written in blood are gone, until the paper is wiped clean.

When the pain begins, spreading from my tongue to my throat and stomach, bright like a fire inside of my body, I wonder if I have made an error. I wonder if this dead letter was not really dead at all.

Or if it was only a soul preserved in words, waiting for a willing host; as the pain continues, as it flares inside me, the words on my skin seem to glow and shift. I wonder if this is one letter that should have stayed dead.

But now he will live on inside of me.

12

Take thy beak from out my heart, and take thy form from off my door!'
Quoth the raven, `Nevermore.'
From **The Raven** by Edger Allen Poe

i

It had always been this way.

He sat at his desk, the light of the monitor the only source of illumination. The room around him was filled with dark shapes. To him, they moved in the shadows.

The wind whistled outside of his window. To others, it would seem like it was singing. To Oliver, the wind sounded like a banshee screaming at him. He shivered and closed the window a bit more.

Giving the window an angry glance, as if admonishing it for letting the air inside in the first place, Oliver shuffled back to his desk and stared at what he had written.

As always, he thought that his work was quite possibly the worst thing he had ever put to paper. He always thought this. It didn't matter though, he always continued writing. The stories kept him going. He wrote as if he were possessed, sometimes going without sleep, sometimes without food.

Outside, the world around Oliver kept passing him by.

He knew that it was doing this, but he had ceased to care. He interacted with the world so little now that he had given up, he had compromised. He had conceded. He interacted only with the stories he wrote, the people that he put on paper. He dealt only with those that he had created.

His stories couldn't talk back to him. They were all he had left. They were all that remained, more words trapped in his head, wanting to be born onto paper, virginal and white, the ink like blood striking its shape boldly on the page, coming to life before his eyes.

His stories never burned him, never hurt him and only occasionally made him uncomfortable. He could deal with the world, his world, his way. . To him, his writing was like a quest. He had always wanted to be a somebody. Now, as death approached him, he finally would be. After he died, he would have left a mark in two ways. And both came back to words.

They called him The Raven.

As a sixty five year old man, Oliver found himself at quite a disadvantage. He had only a scant few years remaining. He intended to enjoy them the way he wanted to, even if it meant keeping everyone he loved out. Even if it meant teaching people to respect the balance that life craved. Sometimes, it was a *hard* lesson.

Oliver knew that the outside world was filled with bright things. It was filled with things that could entice wonder and beauty. But it could also hurt, lashing out with its cruel fingers.

In everything, Oliver knew, there was balance.

The world outside was filled with garlands and trees bright with lights that glittered like stars, wrapped along the branches, the brightness rustling amongst the dead leaves. There were carollers in the streets, small children with their smiling, bright happy faces and their rosy pink cheeks.

The world would be filled with banks of snow, people carrying overpriced presents that gave the economy a boost as everyone spent more then they had, always living on gluttony, living outside their means.

The puppets were never satisfied with what they had. They always had to grasp for what eluded them instead of cherishing what they had.

The world would be filled with fake joy and cheer that no one felt anymore, not really. No one is ever completely happy, not really. Not to the tips of your fingers and toes happy. You would only feel that once in your life, at the very moment of your death.

Life played a cheap trick, keeping the very thing you seek most from you until the moment you pass away. Life, in short, was a fucking Christmas. He didn't think of what he wanted to do as murder. Instead, he thought of what he needed to do as a gift. He would be a bringer of joy this year. He would give people what they sought the most.

He came every year. It had always been this way.

"Merry fucking Christmas." Oliver whispered.

It had always been this way.

They had given him the name. In a way, "The Raven" suited him perfectly. Some would argue that he was a monster, something to be feared. Oliver thought of himself as something different, something good, in a way. He saw himself as a bird of prey, pecking out the darkness to make bright stars.

But he didn't give himself the name. He didn't want the prestige of a title. To Oliver, it was all about balance.

If he was going to give joy to others, he had to leave a sign. There were some that came to him to die, that knew how to look for the signs. They had to learn something about themselves to earn the gift.

But they all learned in the end.

12 had always been the number. It was the one that had called to him again and again, for there must be a balance in all things. There must be some sort of symmetry to life. There were rules.

It had always been this way.

For eleven years he had chosen 12 people. Sometimes it was random; sometimes there was a common thread to all of their stories, a certain thread that they would find if only they could stop to pick their situations apart.

The meat puppets were so fascinating to him, so delicate in their movements, yet so fierce in their will to survive. But when the joy filled them with its release, they stopped resisting.

Only *then* could they experience *true* joy.

True, the ones he helped achieve bliss were often the vagrants of society, but this was the way of things. And, in giving out balance, he gave to those that were depraved and in need of saving. They were the ones who had stepped off the beaten path, the ones who had gone to hide in the darkness.

He brought them out; he took them out from the darkness and into the limelight. They were dead by the time they achieved their fame, but in this way he assured each of them that their life would stand for something, that it would be marked in some way.

As his life would, in turn, be marked by them.

Oliver knew that he lived in a world full of balance. There had to be control. Those who had nothing would appreciate the joy the most. Those who had nothing were the most grateful.

If he did not give the joy to the needy, the story would play out differently. It didn't matter what he did, didn't matter how many times he had plotted it, they continued to surprise him. He thought of them as puppets, no more than things to do with as he pleased. Yet there was something in them that continued to pull at him. There was a richness to their skin that he would never achieve, and a fullness to their lives that he would never grasp.

There must be balance, Oliver thought.

At first, the idea of what he had become, of what he had allowed to happen, sickened him. After the third year (everything happens in threes, after all,) something within Oliver changed. Something clicked.

Reaching forward, Oliver took a slim white tipped cigar out of a thin silver case. His shaking hand lit the tip of the cigar and it flared, bright with light in the darkness of the apartment. Oliver's eyes were momentarily blinded by the bright flash and he wished again that he had taken control of his life when he had been younger.

He took a drag off of his cigar, the smoke clogging his throat, leaving him momentarily breathless. He pushed the smoke out with a soft, limp breath. The smoke was sweet on his tongue.

"There's no time for that now," Oliver said. "Needs must." His voice was hoarse in the darkness. He felt a momentary pang, wishing that there was someone to hear his words. But then another blast of anger pushed this down. There was no one. It had always been this way.

This was the way of things. He took in a mouthful of smoke and moved his tongue around as if savouring it. Oliver's brown skin smelled of cigars and wine. A puff of smoke began to fill the room around him, the whiteness of it pale against the shadows of the room.

Oliver knew that it had all been coming up to this. He knew that after 12, there could be no more. He hoped that, after his task was complete, whatever was in him would let him go.

There was a part of him didn't want to let go, not yet. Not after so long. After the third, the fifth, the seventh, and the ninth, the feeling began to increase, a heady sense of want and need that filled him completely.

Inside his head, these feelings railed at him constantly. They screamed and moaned beneath his skin, invading his private moments, invading his dreams. The only way to keep them quiet was to write, to let what words came to him pour out onto the page. It was the only way he could appease them.

And there was the 12. The eleven before it were gifts, the voices inside of him, remnants of those he had chosen and quieted for a handful of days by the gift of blood. This one was for him. The end for Oliver was coming and he intended on collecting.

12 would be his reward.

iii

The snow crunched under his careful steps.

To Oliver, it sounded like shards of broken glass splintering under his feet. He had never understood how snow could be perceived as being magical. The snow sounded to him like dreams being shattered. If he could, he would make the world silent. There was far too much noise in the world.

There was far too much noise within him. He winced as one of the voices inside his head became particularly loud. They were always louder before the blood. They were as hungry and desperate as he was.

Shaking his head, Oliver tried to focus on the task at hand, on the game that he had been playing.

He had everything that he needed in a small rucksack that was strapped to his back. He could hear the items inside the bag making noise and he walked slower. He was in no hurry to reach his destination. That was part of the anticipation, part of the game.

The game had already begun. Twelve years ago, to be exact. And tonight it would finally end for him, finally cease to be. Oliver wondered what his life would be like without the game, but chose not to dwell on these thoughts for now.

He had more important things on his mind.

Oliver wondered about the method of this one, how he would complete it. He didn't know if he had it in him, but he would have to try. She knew that he was coming for her. It was the beginning of the end and he had to grasp for the strength to complete it.

In his rucksack Oliver had a few select items: a slim volume of the poem "The Raven" by Edger Allen Poe, a sharpened quill, its tip a dark sleek metal. He stopped to make sure that he had his journal and his writing pen. He did. Inside the journal, tucked within its pages, was a black and white photograph.

Oliver looked at it and wondered about who the person in the photograph had become. He had wondered about her for a very long time. There was still enough compassion left inside of Oliver to feel another momentary pang of pain, deep in his gut. Suddenly it was there no more. He had pushed it aside, as he had always done.

As he approached the house from the outside, going around back to stay out of the view of watching eyes, he could hear music. Oliver thought it was "I'm Dreaming of a White Christmas" by Anne Murray. He fucking hated that bitch. But at least it wasn't Celine Dion. He couldn't stand that bitch either.

Staying in the shadows, Oliver watched her shadow move, long and sleek, over the crust of snow in her backyard. As she moved from room to room, her shadow slunk along the ground as if dancing to the music.

The closer he came to the house, the louder the music became. The song had changed, he was sure of that. "It Came Upon a Midnight Clear." Oliver spared a moment for a smile and looked at his watch.

It was only 9PM, not midnight. In retrospect, he thought that that would have been more poetic. But needs must, he had a long night ahead of him.

So he was early. But then again, he had always been on time for everything in his life. It was better to be early than fashionably late. Besides, he had a lot to do within a short period of time.

Oliver waited until her shadow moved away from the living room and into the kitchen. He waited another heart beat and then slid along the wall towards the sliding door. Quickly taking care of the lock and latch, Oliver let himself inside, his snow covered boots crunching on the carpet.

When she came back into the living room, he was ready. He had the gun out and pointed at her. Oliver witnessed the instant that the fear flared to life in her eyes. He drank in that fear like wine.

"Hello Cynthia," Oliver whispered. "Merry Christmas."

She glared at him, her teeth blue from the Christmas lights on the tree, bright like stars. "I knew you would come for me," she said. Oliver heard no fear in her voice, but he could smell it.

There, underneath the cheap perfume that she wore, a musky smell of warmed milk rose from her skin. As he walked towards her, Oliver breathed it in. He took in the scent of her like he was sipping a fine wine. "Have you missed me?" he asked.

He put the gun inside one coat pocket and removed a silver knife from the other. "Cynthia, I want to write with you. I want to know. Have you been naughty?" His voice deepened. He let the anger that he had held caged inside of him boil, warming his body that had remained so cold for a year.

Oliver only felt human while he was doing the dance. When the blood from the bodies landed on his skin, it sent a shiver through him that made him feel whole. They were puppets, so strong and resilient.

But their flesh was weak.

Cynthia remained silent and Oliver made a noise in the back of his throat. A barking laugh that sounded like the caw of a raven, like a slash of night, sliced through the air. "Did you miss me?" he asked again.

He ran the knife from the tip of her chin down the skin of her neck, the muscles flexing on their own in defence of the intrusion. The human body was incredibly resilient, able to withstand so much pain.

This suited Oliver just fine.

Cynthia's breath began to increase. "Always," she said. Her breath was husky with fear now and Oliver felt himself growing hard. "I have always missed you."

"Liar!" Oliver barked this word, more darkness echoing in his words than before. He made a slash with the knife, the point leaving a small rivulet of blood that ran from her neck to her breastbone. Only skin deep, the blood gleamed like a jewel in the false light of Cynthia's living room. To Oliver, watching as the lights changed from blue, to white, and then to red, it looked as if his sister's blood was glowing.

"I want to play a game, Cynthia," Oliver said. "You have a choice. Write or die." He ran the knife softly down the exposed skin of her left arm, the blade whispering.

Cynthia tried to control the shaking in her body. "Please, Oliver. I loved you once." She looked him with bleak eyes. "Please, Oliver." She let out a small sob. "Please."

Oliver regarded Cynthia with cold eyes. "Begging already?" He leaned forward and licked a tear that slid down her cheek.

"I expected better of you. We can't be at the begging portion of our holiday festivities already, can we? Why are you crying?" he whispered. His voice was as soft as cream. This was the voice that Cynthia knew and feared. Cynthia flinched as if he had touched her. "I haven't even written anything yet."

"Make your choice," he said.

iv

When Cynthia woke, Oliver had everything ready. He had gone to great lengths to make sure that he had done everything properly. No one relished creativity any more, in any art form. No one stopped to admire the beauty that was all around them.

Instead, they were only focused on who *they* were, what *they* wanted. They didn't really *need* anything. That was the sad part to Oliver. He had never witnessed so much waste, so much destruction.

And he *abhorred* both.

Oliver found it interesting and somewhat compelling. Every time he began to feel a moment of remorse for what he had done, what he had started, he would listen to the news on the radio and what he heard would anger him for days.

Millions of people out there in the world killing themselves for no reason, teenage girls joining cults, celebrity marriages, the perfect recipe for holiday fruit cake; as if anyone eats that shit anymore anyway.

If Oliver were asked to pick his least favourite food in the entire world, it would be Christmas fruit cake. He remembered it as a child, full of odd bits and bobs, reeking of rum. The icing on the top, white and gooey (probably marzipan, he thinks).

The icing tasted funny and he always had a nasty stomach ache afterwards. With the amount of booze he'd ingested as a child, it was a wonder he hadn't become an alcoholic.

Everyone drank at Christmas time. They liked to rile it up for the holidays. On some evenings, when nothing else would entertain him, Oliver would sit in his living room and listen to the world around him. He would listen to the drunken fools carolling like whores in the street.

Noise bothered him. He tried to keep everything quiet, but you couldn't keep everything out. In the end, he had learned to live with the noise, learned to live with the racket.

His psychologist at the time had been thrilled. His shrink had said that Oliver was making great progress.

Well, I showed him, Oliver thought. In the end, to quiet the noise around him, Oliver simply started removing the problem, one person at a time. It was a simple matter of how hard you were willing to work for what you wanted in life.

And Oliver worked very hard.

He turned when Cynthia began to stir. Oliver heard the clanking and knew that she had begun to wake up, that she was aware of what was about to happen. There was something to be said for having them alive when he wrote; it did something to the blood. When Cynthia began to whimper, Oliver knew that she had seen the tools that he had laid out. She had seen the small black book of poetry that shone darkly in the half light of the room.

He turned and looked into her pleading eyes. They were huge eyes, cartoon eyes that seemed to fill her entire forehead.

Beneath the gag that he had tied around her mouth, and the nine layers of duct tape that he had put overtop of her mouth, neck, and chin, she made a loud moaning noise. Some of the sound came out of her nostrils, like a forgotten echo.

"Oh Cynthia," Oliver whispered. "You know that there's no use in begging. You brought this on yourself, you know. You really did."

Walking slowly towards her, Oliver let himself feel a momentary thrill that blew against his spark of anger. The spark flared into a fire and Oliver wondered if his eyes were glowing; the heat came off of him in waves, anger that was twelve years old.

Cynthia moaned out two vague shapes of sound. Oliver knew what she had said right away, when someone else might have never been able to understand.

"Kill you?" Oliver laughed. "Why, my dear, would I want to do that? Don't you know how much fun we're going to have, you and me, together?"

Standing in front of her, Oliver looked down at Cynthia with dark eyes, twelve years of hate burning in them. "I want to write with you,

Cynthia." He moved away from her. "But you don't want to write? You've already made your choice?"

v

Cynthia was whimpering in earnest now.

If not for the gag and the duct tape, her howl would be piercing his ears by now. But he needed her to be quiet. A squealing pig brought more pigs; this was always a good rule to live by.

Looking into her eyes, Oliver was pleased to find that they had turned glassy and full. Tears slid down her cheeks, leaving track marks along her face. Oliver approached Cynthia and smiled almost kindly.

"It does no good to cry now, Cynthia. You knew what you were doing, what you did." He plucked the black and white photograph from his pocket and showed it to her. Her eyes widened still further when she saw the photo.

She knew what it meant.

"Do you remember that day, Cynthia? I remember. It was the day you took everything from me, the day that the 12 began."

Cynthia mumbled something behind her gag and Oliver was curious despite himself. He knew that he had a lot of work to finish up this evening, but he wondered if he should give her the chance to speak. Learning forward, he ripped off the duct tape in one fluid motion and unwrapped the cloth that was around her mouth. He also removed the rolled up sock that he had shoved in her mouth to dampen most of the noise.

For a few moments, the room around them was filled with the sound of Cynthia's sobbing. Humans were so strong, so resilient, yet so prone to weakness. Oliver saw this all the time in his line of work. When fear set in, strength left human bodies in a rush, leaving the body nothing but a shell for strong emotions.

Cynthia let out several wet sobs before Oliver reached forward and slapped her roughly across the face. The sound of the slap reverberated in the small room, the stone walls seeming to hold in the echo long after the slap was over.

It had the desired effect. Cynthia sat quietly, looking at him with eyes that, even now, pleaded with him. Oliver chuckled softly. "You were always one to turn on the waterworks," he said softly.

"Oliver, you can stop this," Cynthia said. "You can stop this now, you can stop this and we can both walk away, and we don't ever have to see each other again." A sob forced its way out of her mouth and she drew in a deep breath. "I won't *tell* any*one*. I *promise* I *won't* tell."

Oliver's laughter deepened. When he could speak again, he looked at her with narrowed eyes. "Like you wouldn't tell before? Like you didn't tell anyone? Like you didn't sit there on the witness stand and tell them all what I did?"

Cynthia let out another muffled sob. "That was a long time ago."

Oliver slapped her again. "Don't patronize me," he said. Though he was only whispering, the sound of his voice echoed around the room. Blood had already dripped from the ties at Cynthia's wrists

89

and ankles. He couldn't see the blood, not yet. But he could smell it.

"You were always a shitty liar, Cynthia. But you know that." As he spoke, he began to stuff the sock back in her mouth and retie the gag around her mouth, despite her sobs of protest.

He looked into her eyes as he put new duct tape over her mouth. "Where I come from, there are penalties for a woman who lies." He stood back and regarded her. He smiled, almost as if they were talking about the weather. "My pen has run dry." Oliver leaned in closer and licked another tear off of her cheek.

"I need some ink, Cynthia," he said.

vi

Cynthia's sobs, hesitant to begin with, increased in volume when Oliver removed the scalpel from the inside pocket of his coat. He cut her first underneath her chin, starting near her jaw and working the scalpel down in one fluid moment. Blood began to flow freely from the wound. There would be more before the night was over.

"I'm really disappointed in you," Oliver said, watching as the blood from her wound began to soak her shirt. "I expected better of you, Cynthia." He went to the tray of tools he'd laid out and picked up one that was almost hidden amongst the others.

It looked like a fountain pen. It was sleek and made out of a dark wood. But there was no well for ink; this was an old fountain pen that Oliver had found at a rummage sale. He had recognized it for what it was right away. It was a fountain pen that required its own supply of ink.

Over the years, he'd had the nib sharpened to a fine edge. Testing it now, he watched as blood welled on the pad of his thumb. He licked the beads of blood off of his thumb with his tongue and tasted iron and mineral and the promise of more.

When he picked up the small black book, Cynthia's whimpers reached new levels of volume. It didn't matter now and wouldn't matter until they were done. Oliver did what he could to drown out her noises. Besides, he had work to do.

He stood before her and put the fountain pen and the black book to the side. There was one final thing that he would have to do. He had tied her hands to the chairs arms, but had removed the back of the chair. There was nothing holding her upright except her spine - for now.

With calculated movements Oliver went to a drawer in his workstation and took out a metal collar. Being careful to avoid the wound that still bled on her throat, Oliver attached the metal collar around Cynthia's neck. Going to his workstation again, he took out a long length of chain.

He attached one end of the chain to a set of pulleys and attached the other end through a loop in the collar that he locked to the chain. Cynthia's eyes asked him a question. "What is the chain for?" she said.

Walking to his workstation once more, he pressed a button on one of the pulleys and the chain started to clink up, link by link, so that eventually the chain held Cynthia upright. "I don't want you falling over because you're weak from blood loss. You would wreck my concentration that way."

With an almost clinical detachment, Oliver ripped off Cynthia's shirt. She wore no bra underneath but it wasn't her bitty titties he was interested in. Not anymore.

"When you told, when you blabbed, you brought your own death to your doorstep." Oliver ran a finger along one curl of blond hair that had fallen onto her face. "Did you know that? In the end, I am but the puppet, just like you, giving you the death you so richly deserve."

Picking up the fountain pen and the slim black book, Oliver moved behind Cynthia to look at her naked back. It would be his canvass, his virgin page of skin.

When she bled, however, she would bleed words.

vii

Oliver took out an antiseptic wipe and with a gentle hand wiped Cynthia's back clean of sweat and grime. "Do you remember me telling you that I had to write to keep them quiet?" Oliver asked Cynthia. "Do you remember me telling you that?"

Tears sliding down her face, sobs wracking her throat behind the gag, Cynthia nodded, even though her body was held upright by the metal collar. Oliver pulled on soft leather gloves. He had considered latex gloves when he had begun his work twelve years ago, but had almost immediately dismissed them. They seemed too cold, too impersonal.

"In a way, it's you that I have to thank," he said. "You were the one who helped me to find my writing."

Cynthia let out a sob and Oliver slapped her on the back of the head, sending some of her blond tresses flying. "You don't make a sound," Oliver said. "I don't want to hear anything from you. Not anymore." Resisting the urge to stab her with the fountain pen, Oliver slapped her on the back of the head once more.

"I wrote so that I would not go crazy. When you told, when they took her away from me, when you testified against me, I had to write so that I wouldn't go crazy. You can see how that would work, don't you? Trying to fill my head with words so that they could drown out the voices?"

"I loved my daughter." His voice had deepened again and Cynthia knew that the rage was out now, that there would be no putting it back, no twisting on the top of the jar to keep it in. "I loved her more than I loved you. I would never have done the things you said I did." He spat on her, the glob landing limply in her blond curls. "Never."

He licked the end of the nib with his tongue, relishing the taste of blood that was left there, and pressed it against her skin, creating shapes that would form syllables.

"What my daughter and I had was love. We couldn't help what we had between us; I couldn't help how she wanted to express her love. But I never touched her inappropriately. I never took anything she did not want to give."

As he worked, blood began to drip down her back and he wiped it away with his leather glove. Twelve lines, he thought. It always came back to twelve. To *12*.

"I had to take her from you. Surely you understand that, even after all this time. If I couldn't have her, no one could. Don't you see that it's what she would have wanted?" Cynthia gave only a brief sob in reply as he cut into her skin once more.

Four lines in, he thought; eight more lines to go. He wrote in an elegant hand, full of curling letters. It was only appropriate, considering the author.

Oliver didn't think of what he did as plagiarism. The author of the very words was dead, after all. At home, he wrote his own words; out here, in his work, he quoted Poe's. The skin of the puppets was no place to gauge the reaction of the reading public to his own work. He had only one slate with which to convey his message.

There were only 12. There could be no misunderstandings. It had always been this way. They called him The Raven because of the words he carved into other's skin. What they did not know was that his word choice had nothing to do with birds. He chose "The Raven" because it was a man's lament for what he had loved, for who he had loved. Lenore. 12 always came back to Lenore.

It was always this way.

He looked at the lines that he had etched into his sister's skin, the blood gleaming like jewels in the half light of his special room. Tracing his finger over the words, he recited them out loud, knowing them well enough from memory:

Once upon a midnight dreary, while I pondered weak and weary,
Over many a quaint and curious volume of forgotten lore,
While I nodded, nearly napping, suddenly there came a tapping
As of some one gently rapping, rapping at my chamber door.

Four lines. Four lines that said so much that multiplied to eight, which multiplied to 12, always to 12. As Cynthia gave out another sob, he shushed her and ran a hand through her hair in comfort.

"You should be proud," Oliver said. "You will finally be a work of genius, a piece of a bigger puzzle. Your life will finally have *meaning*, Cynthia." He leaned in and kissed the back of her neck like he had used to. "It's something your life didn't have, and what greater gift could there be than bringing worth and meaning to the holiday season?"

viii

As Oliver worked, Cynthia slipped in and out of consciousness.

When she was finally still, he had only completed eight of the twelve lines that he needed to leave. As he worked on the rest of the words, carving them out of his sister's skin like afterthoughts, Oliver wondered once again why those he loved betrayed him. Like 12, it had always been this way.

As he worked, as he wrote, Oliver floated out of his body as he always did at this time during his work, during 12. Although the words had been written by someone else a century ago, they seemed to come from somewhere inside of him, as if he were channelling them instead of merely quoting them.

When he was done, he took a deep breath and looked at the lines he had written:

Once upon a midnight dreary, while I pondered weak and weary,
Over many a quaint and curious volume of forgotten lore,
While I nodded, nearly napping, suddenly there came a tapping,
As of some one gently rapping, rapping at my chamber door.
`'Tis some visitor,' I muttered, `tapping at my chamber door -
Only this, and nothing more.'

Ah, distinctly I remember it was in the bleak December,
And each separate dying ember wrought its ghost upon the floor.
Eagerly I wished the morrow; - vainly I had sought to borrow

*From my books surcease of sorrow - sorrow for the
lost Lenore -
For the rare and radiant maiden whom the angels
named Lenore -
Nameless here for evermore.*

Always the same lines, always the same. It had always been this way. When he carved the name Lenore into his sister's back, his hands were shaking.

Taking a deep breath, he calmed himself and looked at his daughter's name shining in blood on pale white skin.

In this way, he would remember his daughter.

Cynthia began to stir then and Oliver smiled. The last bit of his work was the most important and he always preferred it when they were still alive in the end.

Moving around to her front so that she could see him, Oliver smelled the fear rising off of Cynthia's skin in waves. He tasted her fear on his tongue and swallowed it, savouring the taste. Cynthia was still moaning behind her gag when he put the nib of the fountain pen to her neck.

With a swift motion, he pulled the sharpened nib of the pen across her throat. He was rewarded for his efforts with a flow of blood that slipped out of her skin, soaking her already blood-wet shirt.

As Cynthia gurgled out the last breaths of her life, Oliver thought about all the work that he still had left to do. It was the thirteenth of December and Christmas was now twelve days away. 12.

Always 12. As Oliver cleaned up the blood that marred his pristine tools, he touched Cynthia's face one final time, letting his fingers move a strand of hair away from her oval face.

"Merry Christmas, Cynthia," Oliver whispered. "And have a happy new year, you fucking bitch."

He gathered his tools and left the room, leaving the corpse of his sister behind him like a piece of forgotten punctuation.

ix

The snow crunched under his feet, yet to Oliver it no longer sounded like the shards of broken dreams, the small ecstasies of yesterday.

Instead, now that 12 had ended, the crinkle and crackle of the snow underneath his shoes sounded to him like music. It seemed to be racing him on.

Oliver wondered vaguely what tomorrow would bring. He had decided this year that he would let something else choose the chosen this year. He had decided to give himself gifts.

For if he was a giver of gifts, a giver of joy, shouldn't he receive gifts and rewards for a job well done? This year he would let the fates decide on their whim. He would let the winds of chance blow them into his path.

It had not always been like this.

Oliver had begun to do something that he had never done before. He was sixty seven years old. His body was old and shrivelled and the cancer filled him from top to bottom. But what if he lived?

What if he lived beyond the year they gave him? What if the cancer didn't kill him?

What would happen then?

It had not always been this way. But he wondered if he should start a new tradition.

With the snow crunching under his feet, the warmth of Cynthia's blood still on his skin, the sound of carollers in the distance and the sated but still hungry voice in his head, it was no wonder that Oliver wasn't paying attention.

He saw bright spots of red as the woman's packages and bags went flying. There was a delayed moment, a breath caught in time, and Oliver felt air leave him in a gush.

When he had straightened himself and stopped the woman from falling, Oliver looked at the woman the hand belonged to.

He was looking into the face of an angel.

x

The woman cursed. "Shit," she said. She said it with a small grimace. "Sorry. You know, it's the last fucking thing I need around the holidays."

The woman was older. Oliver couldn't tell in this light, but he knew that she was at least forty-something. He could see wisps of blond and white hair peeking out from underneath her cap. Light blue eyes that almost matched his own in colour regarded him. He wondered if he was imagining the twinkle he saw there. Her face stirred something in the depths of his mind. She reminded Oliver of someone, but he could not place the name or the face. She looked familiar to him but he could not say why this was.

When Oliver said nothing, she shrugged. "You ever get to the point where you want to punch the next fucking caroller who comes to your door in the face?"

Oliver laughed at the woman's brutal honesty. "You have no idea." He wiped a tear away from his eye and held out a gloved hand. "I'm Oliver."

She took his hand in a firm but gentle grip. Looking at him, she smiled. "I'm Lenore," she said. "Merry fucking Christmas."

Oliver smiled and felt a warmth inside of him for the first time. "Oh, my *dear*." His voice was a soft croon. "I think we're going to get along just fine."

He helped her gather up her fallen packages and bags, and then took her hand. "Can I buy you a nightcap?" he asked.

Lenore smiled at him. There was kindness within the hard slash of her lips. "As long as you're buying."

Holding her hand in his, Oliver walked towards the shadows of the night, letting the darkness claim him.

And waited for tomorrow to come...

The Door Without

"Mad Hatter: "Why is a raven like a writing-desk?"
"Have you guessed the riddle yet?" the Hatter said, turning to Alice again.
"No, I give it up," Alice replied: "What's the answer?"
"I haven't the slightest idea," said the Hatter"

Lewis Carroll, *Alice in Wonderland*

i

He thought of himself as a historian, of sorts. At least that is what he had become.

He sat, he listened, he recorded. That was all that he was really required to do. But it all started with, like many things, a Door.

Didn't Alice open a door to walk into Wonderland? Yes, there was that tumble down the rabbit hole, but that was just a silly metaphor. The real meat of the thing was the door itself.

When he had moved into his present home, some years ago been connected to the ones next door. There was a small shat that ran between the basements of both houses, a heating vent that provided circulation. Supposedly, it was common in the day.

However, a week before he had bought his house, the door had been sealed. It was still there,

101

its cold metal flaked with rust and aged paint. The door reminded him of something like a bomb shelter's. Unfeeling, yet necessary.

His next door neighbour had been an older woman. But she had a younger son, a small boy child. He had heard the boy, even if he had never seen him-Cedric had never laid eyes on the boy.

He thought of the boy, now, however.

When the old woman had died, he had sealed the door. The neighbours on the street said the old woman had died of heartbreak, when her boy had gone missing. Even so, he thought it best to seal the door there-besides, it would save him a ton money on the new house. He was heating her basement for nothing.

For reasons he couldn't explain, he had taken his writing desk down there, this old mahogany thing. His office normally sat inside his living room, just off from his kitchen. However, when the door was sealed, he had moved his desk downstairs. Or rather, hired movers to do it. It came to the same thing really.

He kept a gap between the door and the desk. There was something, in his mind, that compared putting something up against it something he was ashamed of. Did the closure of heat to an empty house give him a moment's unrest? No. Did he remember the dead?

Yes.

So out of respect for the old woman and her boy, he had left the door bare and visible beside him. The desk had been pushed up against the wall, waiting sentry beside him on the wall. He had filled the area with Christmas lights, to take away from the flat darkness of the basement. No matter how well lit, the door remained in the shadows.

He left it there and wrote anyway. At first, his stories were darker than normal, a tinge frightening. He had moved away from writing more comedic adventures to writing something a little darker.

Cedric's agent was thrilled. "I'm so happy that you've decided to do something different." Kyla Rivere breathed a sigh of relief into the phone. "I didn't want you to get typecast as a comedy slapstick writer." She mused. "Look at what happened to that poor Evonavich woman." She clicked her lighter over the phone and he heard her taking in a drag off of her cigarette. "Ghastly, really."

"So you like it?" Cedric had to admit that he was nervous about the book he had written. It was a macabre tale of a man in a lonely Victorian house, waiting for his lost love. When she returns, she is different than he suspects her to be. He normally wrote about people getting into situations that involved a narrow escape and a few laughs. Not some man waiting for his bride to come home. He had never written a fucking historical, for fuck sakes and that's exactly what The Door Within was.

"Like it? Darling, I fucking love it. The women will fucking wet themselves when they read this. Where did you come up with a name like Harold Buttermore? Fuck it, we can change it in edits, Ced Darling. We need something that'll make the women cream in their pants.

"Must you be so graphic?"

"I'm the thinker, you're the writer, honey. It's what I do. What do you think of Henry and Cenise, Darling?"

"For what?"

"For the name changes, Darling. Isn't Cenise beautiful?"

"Why do heroine's have to have suck funny names?"

"It's what sells, Darling. We'll talk about it in edits. This could be the start of a series, couldn't it?" There was a hunger in her voice that Cedric had never heard before. "You left it kind of open ended there."

Cedric thought for a moment. Really, he was listening. It was like he had been told the story of Harold and and Lois Buttermore, as if someone had whispered it inside of his head. He thought and listened. "Possibly, yes, three books, each a different generation of the family."

"Excellent, Darling!" Kyla sounded thrilled. "We'll do a three book release this year."

"This year?" Cedric's bowels kind of drenched with panic. "That's like three books in one year."

"Yes, Darling, I know that. I can count you know. The thing is, this is rather shorter and slimmer than you're usual work. Why not have three shorter books come out and then do an omnibus release? We could do a serial thingy, make that popular again."

"Always the bottom line with you, huh?"

"Yes, Darling. I thought you'd figured that out by now. There's always a way to spin it. You're the whiz kid, I'm the money maker. I work, you create."

"Yes, Dear." He said.

"I smell New York Times with this, Darling! Gotta run, kiss kiss."

The click in his ear had been final but soft.

ii

To Cedric's great surprise, it was.

His novel, what became *Waiting for Cenise* did well-very well in fact. Kyla had phoned him with the news. "You did it, you handsome stallion, Darling!"

Cedric was tired and the morning had come early. His evenings were becoming steadily greyer, steadily longer. He wasn't sleeping very well. He had written so much that his finger tips throbbed as if they were bleeding. Sometimes, Cedric checked for blood on the keys of his laptop. Thus far, there were none. "What the fuck do you want?" Cedric said. "I've been writing for days. I've already sent you *Keeping Hawthorne* and I'm working on *The Redemption of Avalane*. It's seven o'clock in the morning. I haven't had coffee."

"You won't need a caffeine rush, Darling! We've hit number one!"

There was the sound of music in the background. "What do you mean?"

"The New York Times, Darling! We made it! *Waiting for Cenise* is number one! I knew you had it in you, you sexy thing, Darling!"

"You're serious?" Cedric lost his breath for a moment. "You're really, seriously, serious?"

"Yes, Darling, you silly old thing." Kyla cackled at him. "Now go and celebrate, Darling. You deserve it. I know I do."

iii

Waiting for Cenise stayed at number one for three solid months. When *Keeping Hawthorne* was released in April of that year, sales for the book doubled that of the first. And copies of *Waiting for Cenise* were selling like hotcakes. Bookstores couldn't keep the books stocked long enough and were running out of copies of both books-they were being bought faster than they could shelf them.

Cedric was in a little bit of a panic. He had gotten to the end of The Redemption of Avalene and didn't know how to finish the fucker. The voices hadn't told him the last part, the very last part.

For his part, Cedric had come to wonder if he had been listening instead of writing. He wondered if, instead of writing his own stories, he had been writing someone else's. The whispers that had clamoured inside of his head had stopped and there were no more words coming.

At first, he thought he was just taking a break. He had two months to go for deadline, hadn't he written two entire novels? Hadn't he written three quarters of the last book? At first, he didn't mind, but now, when he sat down to write, there were no words in him. They were all gone and he wondered if his brain were empty of them.

To Cedric, writing was like breathing. If he could not write, he could not breathe. He often wondered, idly at first and then with growing panic as the weeks grew, if he had just simply lost the will to write. That couldn't be it, though, surely. He had written like a fiend possessed for three months straight.

One night, a week before his deadline, he had a dream.

Normally, Cedric didn't have a problem with dreams. He could control most of them. Some were helpless in their dreams, but Cedric could interact with them. Not this time though. This time, when the darkness came, Cedric knew that he would not move from it until the shadows released him.

iv

The hallway was dark. Everything was dark around him. A staircase swirled into the centre of the floor where his normal stairwell would be. Bright blue carpeting, a robin's egg blue so brilliant it almost shone, covered the steps of a spiral staircase that curved like a snake into the floor.

He didn't want to go down the hole in the floor, along the curving stairs-but he had no choice but to obey. As he stepped on the stairs, one step at a time, each step played a note and

Though he did not want to go down those stairs (no blue could be that natural, he thought), he had no choice. His body moved forward. Though he could not see himself, Cedric knew that he was seeing this, that he was watching, not interacting.

The steps curved around and around and though he was not in control of himself, his dream self still became dizzy. As he went lower along the spiral, each note from each step seemed to ricochet off walls that he could not see. The fear inside him that had started as a seed was a full blown flower inside of him. He wondered idly if vines would sprout from his fingertips.

When he reached the bottom of the spiral staircase, the darkness around him began to recede. When the shadows finally cleared, he saw a woman in front of him. She was clothed in a blue dress with a white apron. Though she should have been a stranger to him, Cedric knew her right away. "Avalene." His dream self muttered.

"Oh, I'm so glad you could come to visit us." Avalene said. Her voice was exactly as he had imagined it: light and full of lilt, like bells being rung. "It's been every so long since we've had visitors. I was saying to Cenise and Hawthorne just the other day that today isn't quite so long as yesterday if there are visitors to receive."

His true self experienced a moment of shock, even as his dream self spoke. He was two people now, the one who was and the one who lived in sleep. "Cenise and Hawthorne? They are here too?"

Avalene smiled at him. "Of course, we are sisters, are we not? Nary a day goes by when we do not lay eyes on each other. Come, I will take you to them. Oh, I do hope you enjoy tea. Cenise makes hers hotter than scalding and Hawthorne makes hers cold as stone, but I will give you a cup of mine, if you wish, kept as warm as summer roses in the sunshine."

Though the girls words were light and airy, Cedric's fear multiplied when she took his hand. Though he knew a dream self could not really feel touch or sensation, he did then. *"This is not possible."* He thought this in his true voice as opposed his dream self speaking the pre-recorded lines of a dream; but Avalene heard him anyways.

She turned to look at Cedric with a mischivious grin. "Oh, anything is possible."

"But this is a dream." He thought.

Avalene giggled, the sound like water over a brook's rocky bottom. "Just because it is a dream does not mean it is any less real. Don't they teach you anything?" She smiled at him and, despite his fear, a moment of warmth flared inside of him. "Worry not, sir. My sisters merely want a word with you, or to give you some words. Yes, that is a more apt description. You have been missing some words, have you not?"

His mind flashed briefly on the last page he had written, a sentence left hanging in the air. Cedric knew he had about fifty more pages to write, knew that the novel was almost done. It was the best thing he had written but he couldn't finish it, couldn't find the words.

Avalene smiled as if she had heard his thoughts. "Yes, words do tend to go wandering if you do not stamp them down onto the page of affix them somehow. Pesky, difficult things, here one moment, gone the next."

They walked onward, Cedric's true self almost floating in his dream self's wake. As they walked, the light that had chased away the shadow began to illuminate the space around him. They came upon a clearing of trees whose leaves sparkled in sunshine. Sitting in the middle of the clearing was a long table set for tea. Though there were many place settings, there were only two women seated there.

Like Avalene, he would have known Cenise and Hawthorne anywhere. Cenise with her blond hair, Hawthorne with her dark hair and Avalene with her blond hair. Though they were supposed to be mortal woman, he wondered if they were something more than that inside of his mind.

They stood as he and Avalene approached the table. "There is our scribe now, sister." Cenise said. Her voice was light as honey and soft as moonshadow. "Did I not tell you he would come?"

"We left him little choice of it, sister." Hawthorne said. "We saw to that."

"Be that as it may, he is here in a dream and without. He has walked through a door within himself so that both of him could be here."

"It is the other door we are concerned about." Hawthorne said.

"Patience, sister, patience. Would you care for some tea, our scribe?"

V

Cedric wondered when his dreams had become so complicated. However, something Cenise said struck a chord with him. "Are you saying I am awake and asleep right now?"

Cenise nodded. "Surely, scribe. How else would anyone really dream? There must be some blood in a soul if the dream is to have any value."

"But souls have no form."

Hawthorne raised an eyebrow at Cedric. "Really? Explain us then. Explain how we live on the page, in the minds of others, in the hearts of readers, yet take on no form whatsoever. We are alive because they wish it so. Does that sound formless to you?"

"Oh, where are my manners?" Cenise said. She took a cup and saucer in hand and poured from a large tea pot. What came out, however, was not tea. Instead, it was words, pouring forth like black alphabet soup, letters and syllables taken from the page by steam or magic.

Cenise held out the cup to him, but she paused a moment. "These are all the words you need." She said. "With these words, you can complete our story and finish your book. It will sell more handsomely than the last two."

"You know of my books?" Cedric asked. He was past being surprised by anything now.

"Who do you think wrote them?" Hawthorne said. "Those voices telling you ideas?

Whose do you think they were? Some random caterpillar blowing smoke circles in your ear?"

"I thought I had come up with them…" Even as he said the words, Cedric knew they weren't true. Hawthorne saw the truth on his face.

"You? You are but the medium, the conduit. You are the vessel in which the words live, but we give them to you, we gift them to you. But we grow hungry and in need."

"Let me know what you need and I will give it to you."

"Aid freely given, we cannot ask for more than that." Cenise passed Cedric the cup and he drank. He expected the words to taste like paper or newsprint, but surprisingly they were full of a rich and heady flavour. The words rushed through his bloodstream like the wind and his fingers already itched to write.

"Now we have given you the ending to our story."

"Why did you withhold it from me?" He whispered. The fright inside of him had grown larger still. It could, in fact, grow roots from his feet, he was sure, right into the ground.

"Nothing comes for free, lovely scribe. Though you tell our story better than we could tell it ourselves, there is always a price to pay for everything." Cenise looked at him, her eyes solemn and grey like storm clouds. "Nothing is free. Nothing."

"I already told you I'd give you whatever you need."

Cenise smiled. "That you did and so you shall. For why not do today what you can do yesterday or tomorrow? We are fortunate that our scribe is so wise."

"What must I do?"

"Why a simple murder, that is all." Cenise said.

vi

Cedric wondered if he had heard clearly. "Murder?" He nearly choked on the word. "Murder is never simple."

"On the contrary." Avalene smiled brightly at him. "Murder is easy, it is living with it that is difficult."

"The woman and her son were lovely, but not enough. We must have a third. There must be a third death. Only then will we be satisfied." Hawthorne's eyes glowed like black ember.

Cedric experienced a moment of sheer panic. "The woman and her son?" His voice was lower than a whisper. "What did you do to them?"

Cenice made a shrugging gesture. "The boy wandered through our door and the old woman came after him. They gave themselves freely to us."

"But they didn't know." Cedric said. "They couldn't have known."

"Never plead ignorance when you open a door." Avalene said. "The beast on the other side of it will sense weakness. You must step over the

113

threshold with a clear heart, otherwise, suffer the consequences."

"What are you talking about?" Cedric asked.

"Why it's what we need, of course." Avalene replied. "What we eat. You didn't think we took their flesh did you? That would be cruel and somewhat barbaric. Besides, I'm not a meat eater."

"Then what *do* you take?"

"Isn't it obvious?" Cenise asked him. "Words, my lovely scribe, words. We cannot live without them. But then, neither can the vessel live without their words. I am told that it is quite a painful process to remove one's words from their mouth." She shrugged again. "But then again, I would not know."

"You want me to give you…a body?"

Hawthorne shook her head. "No, we want you to give us a vessel of words. There is a difference. You will find an adequate vessel and place it in the chamber that lies behind the door in your world. The one you can hear us through. We will do the rest."

"And if I don't get you a…*vessel*?"

"Then the vessel shall be you, lovely scribe." Cenise said, her teeth flashing white and sharp. "Think of all the lovely words that we have poured into you. Think of how lovely you will taste."

She clapped her hands and a striped cat appeared out of thin air as if made of smoke. "You will clasp the cat's tail and he will lead you back to the upper lands. He will show you safe passage."

His true self was no longer in control. Cedric watched as his dream self reached forward to grasp the cats tail. As darkness engulfed him, he heard Cenise utter one final warning. "Take heed scribe. Someone elses words, or yours. But it makes no difference. Bring us our vessel and we will be done with you. Fail to do so and you will wish that words were all we could take from you."

vii

He had wrestled with the notion that the dream had been that, just a dream. However, the door seemed to pulse with need now and he found a tea cup stained with blood on his desk. He knew that, despite the dream being a dream, it had found a foot hold in reality.

Cedric had stared at the cup for hours. Continue as he was and remain as he was or commit murder to achieve fame and finish the bloody story. He wished he had never started writing it in the first place, but if what Cenise had said was true...

In the end, there was only one choice he could make.

viii

And, in the end, it had been relatively easy.

The hooker had put up a minimal fight though she had gotten a few good kicks in. But he didn't really have to kill her, not really, the women would see to her. He just had to get her to the door

115

and through it and close it behind him. He comforted himself with this thought rather than the fact that he was sending a woman to die.

He got her into the house with little trouble, though she had tried to put up a fight when she saw that he mean to take her to the basement. He pushed her and let her fall, though there was one brief moment when he thought she had died. He did not think that the sisters would be happy should their vessel arrive damaged. He thought he read somewhere that all sacrifices must be alive when they are given, otherwise the gift was forfeit.

That's what this was, he realized suddenly. A sacrifice. Hadn't thousands of writers before him offered sacrifices, in one way or another, to achieve the aims of their craft? Hadn't millions of writers sacrificed their own blood to the page in order to tell the tale? So what if he was spilling someone else's? It all amounted to the same thing.

A vessel full of words and blood waiting to be turned into ink on the printed page.

When he got to the bottom of the basement stairs, he saw that she was only knocked out from the fall, though there was a plume of blood that ran along her temple. *What of it*, he thought. *What of it. What was a little blood between words?*

He pulled her over to the old heating duct door. It seemed larger than it had been, perhaps knowing that the body he meant to place behind its keep was larger than that of a child? *It did not matter now*, he thought. *Best to get the deed done.*

There was writing to be done.

116

ix

He pushed his desk away from the door, using the gap that was there as leverage. Though he had it sealed years ago, there was no calking along its edges now. Cedric could feel a draft coming from underneath the door. He wondered whether it came from the house next door or the under world? Or did they amount to the same thing?

Wrenching the door open, he saw only darkness but did smell the faint scent of honeysuckle. He spared the hooker one last glance before shoving her into the dark hole and closing the door behind her. Hearing nothing behind the door, he wondered if he had succeeded.

Then the tips of his fingers began to itch and the voices in his ear grew stronger than they had in some time.

Turning to his computer, he turned on a light to quiet the dark and sat down at his desk. He brought up the manuscript of The Redemption of Avalene, the blank page in front of him gleaming hopefully.

Cedric poised his fingers above the keyboard, his fingers itching madly now and waited for the words to come.

Neverland

"She's quite delusional. I've never seen anything like it."

Dr. Patterson handed me the report on a large wooden backed clipboard. I looked down at the report, started to flip through the pages. "Her name is Wendy Darling?"
Patterson nodded. "She's the eldest daughter of the Darling family. Mister and Missus Darling are quite distraught. The mother blames herself, of course. All the stories she used to tell her as a child."

I scanned the pages of the report. "She thinks she went to some place called Neverland?"

"Yes, where children never grow old. Imagine! She obviously has some issues with growing older and has reverted to a child like state, imagining things that don't exist. I've seen it before; it's quite common in families with a lot of children."

"How many children do the Darling family have?"

"Well, there's Wendy, John and Michael, Wendy being the oldest and Michael being the youngest. Perhaps she's afraid of being replaced by her brothers? Starved for attention and love? There are all sorts of causes to this behavior."

I looked at Wendy Darling through the one way glass. We could see her but she couldn't see us. She sat at a table in the centre of the room, her hands placed primly in front of her, fingers linked, hands still.

She had long brown hair that flowed down past her shoulders framing a heart shaped face. Her skin was rose coloured and she was quite beautiful. Almost too beautiful.

Wendy didn't look around the room, only straight ahead. She smiled then, almost as if she could see us through the glass; as if she knew we were talking about her.

"Have you spoken to her?" I asked.

"Well, that's the strangest thing," Patterson said. "I have and she seems remarkably lucid, as if she's completely sane. Normally the mentally disturbed give off this air of...instability. But Wendy Darling seems really believe in Neverland. She can't be persuaded otherwise."

"She knows we're watching her." I said after a silence.

Patterson looked momentarily flustered. "Inconceivable. There is no way that she could see through the glass."

"Even so, she knows we're talking about her." I said.

"Inconceivable," Patterson said again. But he sounded less certain, unsure.

"I'd like to speak to her. Will there be someone else in the room with me?"

Patterson shook his head. "She hasn't shown a history of violence, only a calm demeanor. So there will be no need. Other doctors who have talked to her have found her pleasant and even charming."

I nodded and looked at her once more through the glass. She raised her right hand in a little wave, wiggling the fingers at me before placing them one more daintily on the table in front of her.

I felt a moment of fear, something not uncommon in my profession, and opened the door to the interview room. Wendy turned to look at me with eyes so blue, it looked as if they were filled with the ocean. They were a bright, brilliant blue; a colour I had never seen before.

"Hello!" Wendy said cheerfully. "Have you come to talk to me about Neverland?" Her voice was bell like, wind chimes being brushed by the wind. It sounded almost like music.

I nodded and held out my hand to her. "I'm Dr. Barrie."

I took my hand in hers and was shocked by its warmth. I was used to the clammy, cold skin of mental patients. Wendy Darling's hands were warm and soft, as if she felt no ill effects at her surroundings.

"I'm very pleased to meet you," she said. "Everyone here has been so lovely to me. I don't know how to thank you."

I said nothing to this. In truth, her brightness made me slightly uncomfortable. I was used to people complaining about the cold, the drafts in the rooms; I was even used to the ramblings of an extremely unstable patient or two. But I had never been thanked by a patient, least of all for their place in a mental facility.

"You're welcome." I said. "I trust that you are feeling well?"

"Oh, very well, thank you. The food here is lovely and everyone is so kind. I feel as if I'm away on a holiday!" She smiled and the smile only heightened her beauty. "Did you want to know about Neverland?"

"Why do you ask that?"

"Because everyone wants to know about it; it's what everyone asks about. No one wants to know about my favourite book or what my favourite food is or what music I like. Everyone wants to know about Neverland."

"Why do you think that is?"

She laughed, that tinkling sound of music. "Because you think I'm crazy. Everyone here thinks it doesn't exist."

"It doesn't."

"How can you be so sure that Neverland doesn't exist? Have you seen it with your own two eyes? Have you ever been there?"

It felt funny to admit that I hadn't been to a make believe place, but I answered her. "No." I said.

"Then how can you tell me that it doesn't exist, Dr. Barrie? Surely you must believe in things that cannot possibly be?"

"I believe in what I can see and touch, no more."

She smiled at me and the smile seemed fairly indulgent. "Oh, Dr. Barrie. So ready to disbelieve, so quick and sure in your resolutions." She reached forward and patted my hand. "Just

121

because you can't see it doesn't mean something doesn't exist."

I stayed silent for a moment, knowing that Patterson would be in the other room, observing the conversation from behind the safety of the one way mirror. I wanted to keep Wendy talking, to hear her voice some more.

"Tell me about Neverland." I asked.

"What would you like to know? There is a lot to tell and I doubt very much I could cover everything in a short conversation."

I rummaged in my brain for a question and asked the first one I thought of. "How do you get there? How do you get to Neverland?"

"Why you fly, of course!" She said this as if it should have been the most obvious of answers.

"Fly?"

"Oh, you don't believe me Dr. Barrie, I can see it in your eyes. But yes, you fly."

"People can't fly Miss Darling."

"Oh, but they can, they can! All they need is a bit of pixie dust."

"Pixie dust?" I felt the conversation was starting to go into some strange territory, one that I was not entirely comfortable with.

"Yes, pixie dust. Oh, and happy thoughts. You must think a happy thought, you can't forget that. That's the most important part." She closed her eyes in concentration and counted the steps on the fingers of her right hand:

"First, you sprinkle yourself with pixie dust. Then you think of your happy thought. It has to be a really happy thought, one that fills you up from your head to your toes. You should feel it tingling in your fingers. Then you begin to fly." She opened her eyes and looked at me. "Well, I think flying is the wrong word. Perhaps the right word is floating. Yes, you float. And you can move yourself in different directions, almost as if you are swimming."

"Flying is like swimming?" I could think of nothing else to say. Hearing her speak had robbed me of all rational thought. As she spoke, I pictured myself floating through the air. I wondered if I needed psychological help instead of Wendy.

"Yes, it's lovely. Complete weightlessness. Then you have to fly towards the second star to the right of the moon. It's best to fly at night so that you can see the stars. You head towards the second star to the right and fly straight on until morning."

She fell silent and I could see it in her eyes that she was reliving every moment, that she was remembering, not imagining, herself in flight.

"Where does one get a pixie?" I asked.

"Why, I haven't the slightest idea." She said. She rewarded me with another one of her smiles. "Peter always has the pixie with him; I've never had to look for one myself."

"Peter?" My interest was piqued, despite myself. "Who's Peter?"

"Why Peter Pan of course! Surely you must have heard of him."

I shook my head. "No, Miss Darling. I haven't."

"Oh, he's lovely, but he's so full of mischief. Sometimes I don't think he will ever grow up. In fact, I'm sure he won't. He's so dead set against it."

"He doesn't age?"

"No one in Neverland does. They remain as they are when they arrived and age not a moment older. There are children that roam the island who would be hundreds of years old here, should they come back." She looked at me with her bright blue eyes; they shone like beacons in the dark room. "I am seventy eight years old."

I laughed before I could stop myself. "I don't believe you." I said. "You don't look a day over twenty years old."

"Oh, but it's true." She said. "Look at my papers, Dr. Barrie, they will tell you the truth."

"I'll do that, Miss Darling."

"Oh, see that you do, Dr. Barrie. I would hate for you to think that I was lying to you. Neverland is such a marvellous place. I almost wish I had never left." A look of sadness crept into her eyes. "Peter must miss me something terribly."

I'm not sure what drove me to do it, but I reached out and clasped her hand. "I'm sure he knows you are alright." I said, hardly believing the words coming out of my mouth. "I'm sure he's waiting for you to return."

Another smile graced her face. "Oh, Dr. Barrie! Do you really think so?"

I nodded, touched by the child like delight in her voice. "I do."

She leaned in closer to me. "I know you're supposed to be persuading me that Neverland

124

doesn't exist, that I'm making it all up. But you've been there before. I can see it in your eyes."

I shook my head. "Impossible, I would have remembered. Besides, I cannot fly."

She laughed again, that wind chime sound. "Dr. Barrie, everyone flies in their dreams. Haven't you ever dreamt of a place more beautiful than any place you've been? A place where your childhood fantasies come true? Where mermaids swim in the water and pirates lay in wait for you?"

Something occurred to me then, a brief flash of memory and dream: A brilliant golden ship floating through the air, the sky black and blue behind it. The clouds parting way for it so that it could make its silent progression through the depths of the sky.

Wendy grinned, a flash of teeth. "Oh, Dr. Barrie. You do remember. Don't you? I can see it in your eyes."

*

"So what did you think of her?"

I turned to see Patterson entering the staff lounge. He had a grin on his face. "Wendy Darling?" I asked.

"Yes," he said. "You believed her, didn't you? You walked out of the interview room so quickly, and you had yet to really delve into her problem. You looked unnerved when you left."

"She…she got to me." I said.

Patterson nodded, agreeing with me. "I will admit that she does have a certain charm, a certain something about her. But surely you agree that it's

125

all nonsense, Barrie? Floating ships and mermaids and people who don't grow a day older? Poppycock," He laughed, a broken cackling sound so different from the tinkling of Wendy's laugh. "Absolute poppycock." He said.

I laughed with him. And as I laughed, I felt as if I were betraying Wendy. Despite evidence that she was crazy, I didn't think she was. I had only spoken to her briefly but she wasn't crazy. I had spoken to mentally disturbed people before and I knew she wasn't that. She wasn't mentally disturbed. She spoke with a clarity and resonance that spoke of sanity. I had no doubt in that.

Wanting to do no more than satisfy my curiosity, I went to the file room and pulled out her file, flipping it open to the first page. I ran my finger down the page, trying to find her date of birth; and then I found it. After a quick calculation, I discovered she was seventy eight. She was seventy eight years old.

I felt a heat begin in my stomach and rise up to my chest. How she could be seventy eight was beyond me, but there was the truth in black and white. Papers could not lie, facts could not lie. I had always depended on fact to prove what was right.

Now I was hoping that fact would prove what was not possible. I thought of something she had said during our brief interview: "Just because you can't see it doesn't mean something doesn't exist."

Without thinking, I grabbed the file and walked down the long tiled hallways to her room. I

knocked on the door and heard no answer. I
knocked again and still heard no answer.

Taking a set of keys from my belt, I
unlocked the door, already knowing that I would
find it empty. She wasn't there.

I felt a momentary pang of loss at her
disappearance. There was so much I still wanted to
ask her, so much I still wanted to know. I looked
around the room again and something caught my
eye.

Sitting on the bed was a small cloth pouch
and a piece of parchment.
Inside the pouch was a glittering substance that
looked like dust. I took a pinch out of the bag and
let it fall from my fingers. It twinkled in the half
light of Wendy's room and dissolved into the air.
With nothing left to do, I stared at the parchment,
taking in the one word printed there in a curving,
spidery script:

Believe.

Potter Head

"We think you have a problem."

I stared around me at the ring of faces. Their features were warped by the low lighting and the flickering of candle flame. "I don't understand what you mean." I said.

My mother, June, looked at me with doe eyes. "No one wants to frighten you, we just have your best interests at heart."

"That's right." Ward said. My father nodded imploringly. A smile was on his face-he never smiled. I knew I was in some kind of trouble. "We only have your best interests at heart."

My brother, Theodore, looked at me, his eyes much like my mothers: Bambi pleading with Flower not to blast his face full of skunk juice. "Listen to us, this is important."

"I still don't understand what this is about." I tried to keep the confusion out of my voice. The remnants of dinner were scattered around the table and the silverware gleamed dangerously, like empty threats waiting to be filled.

"It's about…" My mother began. "Well, it's about your addiction." The pearls she wore around her neck blinked at me like eyes.

I blinked at her. "My addiction?" I repeated. "I'm not addicted to anything."

"It's about your…Harry Potter addiction, son." My father said. Ward looked at me with a calm face, as if by projecting a serene outlook, I would not feel threatened.

"This is about Harry Potter?" I asked. I let out a short bark of a laugh. "Harry Potter is not an addiction." I said.

"I've done some research," Theodore said. "On the internet. There are others out there like you." He reached out and took my hand. I resisted the urge to take it back. "There are lots of Potter Heads out there." He patted my hand reassuringly. "You're not alone you know."

"But I'm not addicted to Harry Potter." I said. "He just brings me joy."

"You do know that Harry Potter isn't real, don't you son?" Ward looked at me with his sad, puppy dog eyes.

"Of course I know he isn't real." I said. "The books bring me joy," I said. "That's what I meant, the books bring me joy."

"We think you may be addicted to Harry Potter." June said.

"How can books be an addiction?" I asked her. "It's more of an obsession, really, more than anything."

I thought of the different editions of the books I had (both UK and American) and the editions of the books I had with the adult covers. I thought of the newly released paperback editions I had, their new white covers soft and gleaming.

It was more than just the books, though. I had a Time Turner necklace that hung side by side with a Gryffindor crest and a replica of Harry's Wand. One wall of my bedroom was taken up with a poster for the second movie, Harry Potter and the Chamber of Secrets. I thought of the mug I drank coffee out of every morning, emblazed with the Hogwarts School of Witchcraft and Wizardry Crest.

I had Harry Potter lego that stood on my desk and I would move Hermione around in a different position every day. I had several Harry Potter games for my Nintendo DS and, more often than not, I would be playing one of them.

I thought of the tattoo I had of Harry's scar that graced his forehead but instead graced my right wrist. I looked down at it now and held it self-consciously.

"Alright," June looked at me. "Let me ask you a few questions. Then we can determine whether or not you are addicted." She said. "And I want yes or no answers, your honest answers."

"Alright." I said.

"Do you think you could go a week without talking about Harry Potter?"

"No." I said. "Probably not."

"Do you think you could go a week without reading any of your Harry Potter books?"

"No." I said. I didn't like where this was going.

"Do you think you could go a week without playing one of your Harry Potter games or watching one of the Harry Potter movies?"

I thought of my collection of Harry Potter BlueRays and DVD's. "No, probably not."

"Do you think you could go a whole week without even thinking of Harry Potter?"

I looked down at scar tattoo that graced my right wrist. "No, I don't think I could."

"That's an addiction, son." Ward said. "Trust me, I've seen addictive behaviour. Remember that year that I bought all those plaid shorts and played golf all the time?"

Part of my resolve crumpled. "How is that even remotely the same thing?" I asked warily.

"You didn't hear the siren call of those clubs, the lovely green grass, and the flags staked into the wholes, whispering in the wind." He shuddered. "It still gives me nightmares."

"The thing is," Theodore looked at me. "We think you need help. You have a Harry Potter addiction." He took out a notebook from under the table. He had been saving this last part. "There are other Potter Heads out there like you, other adolescents and adults that have become addicted to Harry Potter. Did you know that there are even Harry Potter conferences and conventions?" He shivered. "Imagine."

"The thing is," June said. "We want to help you with your problem."

I stared at them, thoughts of rebellion already coming to me. "I don't have an addiction." I said softly. "The Harry Potter books got me through some tough times." I swallowed, the next part was always hard to admit. "It got me through depression, it got me through three abusive relationships."

131

June's eyes hardened at this. She did not like to talk about these things. "Every time things were too difficult, Harry Potter provided a respite, an escape. Haven't you wanted to be whisked away to a different place and told that you're special? Told that you were a wizard or a witch and all the weird and wonderful things you could do were really magic?"

"Oh, I've looked for that school, Hoggywarts, on the internet." Ward said. "You know that the school doesn't exist, right? That you can't really go there? Apparently they send out letters to let you know you're going." He looked at me imploringly. "You know that you won't receive a letter, right? From this Dumbleydore person?"

"Of course I know that it's not a real place!" I shouted. I calmed myself. This was not going well. "Of course I know that." I decided to simplify things. "Harry Potter brings me joy." I said softly. "He brings me joy."

"He's not real." June said. She took my hand in hers. "You know he's not real, don't you?"

"Of course I know that." I said. "Of course I do."

But when I looked around at their faces, the candle light flickering and sputtering, casting shadows along their cheeks and brows, I knew that they didn't believe me. June patted my hand, as if something had been decided.

"We want to help you." She said. "So that's why your brother, father and I have put together all the money we have. We're going to get you the help that you need, the help that you need to beat your addiction."

A chill ran down my spine. Now I *really* didn't like where this was going. "What do you mean?" I said. "What are you talking about?"

"There's help out there," Ward said, "for Potter Heads like you." He paused when there was a knock on the front door. Theodore excused himself to go and answer it. He returned with two white suited men, carrying a white jacket.

"What is going on?" I asked. "What did you people do?"

"They're just going to take you to get help." June said as the men grabbed me from either side and shoved my arms into the coat. "They're going to get you the help that you need. But you can be an example to the other Potter Heads." Her eyes shined and this part, I knew, she had rehearsed in her head. "You can be an example to them. You can be their *hero*."

The two white suited men tied the straps, securing my arms behind my back. "But I don't have an addiction." I said. "I don't. Harry Potter brings me joy. He brings me joy!" I was shouting now, screaming at them as the men dragged me down the front hallway and out of the house.

"Don't you understand that?" I shouted. "He was the only thing that brought me joy when times were hard, when times were more than I could bear! That's not an addiction."

"I'm afraid it is." Theodore said. "I've researched it on the internet. But this institution has a new Twelve Step Program for Potter Heads." He paused. "Don't worry, you're going to be cured."

After that, something snapped inside of me. The two white coated men continued to drag me out of the house, to drag me down the front walkway to the white van that was waiting for me, its engine rumbling.

As they opened the back doors, its insides dark like a jail cell, I continued to yell, continued to scream at the top of my lungs. The three of them, Ward, June and Theodore, stood like silent shadows in the doorway to our home.

"He brought me joy! He gave me joy! Harry Potter brings me joy!"

e

Books were dead.

First, eBooks came on the scene. No one seemed to think that they would do very well,. but they boomed beyond anyone's belief. The paper book industry began to shrivel and die like a tree that had lost its leaves.

After those stores, other stores came. These offered your book of choice on an eReader of your choice. It was technological literature at your fingertips, words pouring out like water.

Then it was came eBeams. Devices that would allow you to read one book in less than ten minutes. The device was actually quite simple: a small hand held apparatus that delivered the story into your brain.

Words and phrases would be transmitted through the reader's eyes by infrared lasers in binary code. Once there, the human mind would assemble it into a language that it could understand. You would turn on some music and relax for ten minutes. A whole novel delivered to the brain in digital format.

Karlos didn't know any of this. So when he found the Book, he didn't know what it was. It was tucked underneath the floorboards of his Nana's home. The floorboard, loose and forgotten, lay beside him.

The Book was thick and covered in a green cloth. When he opened this object (for indeed, it seemed to open) pages would fan out at him with something like a whisper. He didn't know what it was - so he brought it to his Nana.

She smiled when she saw it. "Now where did you get a thing like that?" She asked him.

He shrugged and told her. Nana didn't scold him, however. Instead, she patted the red velvet couch beside her. "It's alright, Karlos," she said. "Come here, I won't hurt you." She smiled at him. "I just want to look at it."

Karlos mooved toward Nana and handed her the object. She took it and looked at the title. "Oh, Lady Chatterly's Lover by D. H. Lawrence." Nan lets out a bark of a laugh. "You picked a hot one. Have you read it yet?"

He shakes his head. "It's still on the Restricted eBeam list," he tells her.

Nan's mouth and chin looked like a sour lemon for a moment. "Yes, I suppose it would be." She patted the couch again. "Come here."

Sitting beside her, Karlos smelt her scent of lavender and spice. It seemed to waft from her like secrets that he didnt know. "Karlos," she said, "Do you know what this is?"

He shook his head. "Is it like an eBeam?" He asked. He knew of Lady Chatterley's Lover, he knew of D. H. Lawrence. He knew that he had several eBeams to his credit, but he had never read them.

Nan shook her head. "No, Karlos, this is no eBeam."

"An eBook?"

Nan shook her head again. "No, Karlos, it's kind of like…" She scrunched up her face. "How do I describe this to you? It's…" She struggled for the words. "It's kind of like an old eReader."

Karlos flipped the object over. "There's nowhere to plug in the power cable." He said.

"It doesn't run on electricity or batteries. It's a Book," Nan said.

Karlos shook his head. "I don't understand you," he said. He looked at the Book as if it were a foreign object; and to him, it was indeed such a thing.

Nan sighed. "When I was a young girl, we didn't have eBooks or eBeams or eReaders or eInk. We had Books. We read our stories this way."

"But there are no buttons," Karlos said. "How are you supposed to turn the pages?"

His Nan smiled. "Like this, with your fingers. You take the page like this and turn it, see?" She showed him, and his eyes widened with wonder.

"There are more words!" he said. "More words after that…page?" Karlos looked at her to make sure he got the word right. "But how do the words know how to appear?"

"They were printed this way," Nan said. She touched the surface where the words sat, the story waiting patiently to be read. "On paper."

Karlos's mouth opened in an O shape. "Paper?" He whispered. He had learned about paper in his ancient history class, but had never thought that he would see it. "Can I touch it?" He asked.

Nan only smiled and held the Book out to him. Now that he knew what it was, he reached out almost with reverence. He touched the Paper, brushed his hand along the words.

After a few minutes, he spoke. "Where did the Books go, Nan?"

A pained look crossed her features. "They faded away, like most things do. Technology moved too fast for the written word," she sighed. "It was bound to happen, I suppose."

Karlos reached out a hand to his Nan. He didn't like to see her sad. "It's okay Nan," he said. "With this, we can remember Books." He smiled up at her. "If we remember them, they won't be gone, they will be in here." He touched his head and then his heart.

She leaned down and kissed him on the head. "Such a smart boy."

"Can you read it to me?" He asked.

She smiled. "Normally I wouldn't, as it may be a little old for you. But as you're almost old enough, and you found it, I suppose it can't hurt."

He nestled close to her. He smelled her scent of lavender mixed with the scent of musty paper. It was a heady scent, a scent of the past.

His Nan turned to the first page and read the first paragraph in her soft, lilting voice:

Ours is essentially a tragic age, so we refuse to take it tragically. The cataclysm has happened, we are among the ruins, we start to build up new little habitats, to have new little hopes. It is rather hard work: there is now no smooth road into the future:

but we go round, or scramble over the obstacles. We've got to live, no matter how many skies have fallen.

When Karlos heard sniffling, he looked up from the musty pages of the Book. Tears streaked down Nan's face and she wiped them away with the heel of her right hand.

"Are you okay, Nan?" Karlos asked

She regarded him with glassy eyes and a happy smile. "Oh, don't mind your Nan, Karlos. I'm just being silly. I'm just remembering."

"Remembering what?"

She sighed and closed her eyes for a moment, as if recalling the memory inside of her. When she opened them again, her eyes were filled with wonder. "I was just remembering the first time I read this novel. I was fourteen years old and had to hide it under my floorboards so that my mother wouldn't catch me reading it."

"Why?"

"Well, it was fairly racy for the time. It was even more so when it was first published. Lady Chatterley's Lover was one of the first "romance" novels, Karlos. Books that would depict relationships and relations between a man and a woman."

"But why did you have to hide it?" Karlos asked. "There's lots of sex in the books I read."

Nan chuckled. "There is now, of course. But back then, it was shocking to find a Book that so openly portrayed love between two people. Even more so, this Book is about the love between an older woman and a younger man, something that wasn't talked about openly, much less written about." She stroked the cover of the Book with reverence.

"You remember all that, from reading a few lines?"

Nan nodded. "Its different now, Karlos, where you can literally have a book imprinted in your memory. But in my day, Books were the keeper of memories. I would touch a book on my shelf and remember where I was when I was reading it, who I was with, what the weather was like."

"How can you remember all that from a Book?" He shook his head. "I don't understand."

Nan took his hands in hers. "You're too young to remember a time without eBeams and eReaders. But in the before, any creation, be it a poem or a song or a book or a piece of art, well, they would help us to mark time. They are memory keepers but they were also markers of time. Do you understand?"

Karlos started to nod but then shook his head instead. Nan laughed at his indecision. "It's alright."

Reaching to turn a page, he felt a slight pain and let out a soft cry. He pulled his hand away from the book to see that his finger was bleeding. "It bit me." He said.

His Nan laughed. "Its okay, Karlos, it's just a paper cut. It happens with Books."

"But I've ruined it," he said. "Look, I got my blood all over the pages."

It was true; Karlos' blood had leaked onto one of the pages of the book. Nan looked down at the passage:

What could she do but leave it alone. . .? So she left it alone. Miss Chatterley came sometimes, with her aristocratic thin face, and triumphed, finding nothing altered. She would never forgive Connie for ousting her from her union in consciousness with her brother. It was she, Emma, who should be bringing forth the stories, these books, with him; the Chatterley stories, something new in the world, that they, the Chatterleys, had put there. There was no other standard. There was no organic connection with the thought and expression that had gone before. Only something new in the world: the Chatterley books, entirely personal.

"You didn't ruin it, Karlos." Nan said. Looking down at her grandson's blood, she was struck with an idea. "How would you like to create your own Book Memory?" She asked.

"You mean, put one of my memories inside of this Book?"

"Yes," She said. "Here." She slit her finger along the sharp edge of a page and let her blood drip onto the paper, mingling with Karlos's blood. Then she closed the book and opened it again.

Karlos let out a breath. Their blood had marked the ink there, but the words were still legible. But their blood had created something different on the page, a pattern of lines that stretched out from the centre of the page like leaves, mirrored from one side to the next.

"There," She said. "Now every time we read this book, we will remember when you first found it and when you and I read it together. In that way, we will remember."

Saying nothing, Karlos nodded. He seemed to treat the moment with reverence. Nan smiled down at him and ran a hand through his dark hair. "Would you like to read some more?"

He nodded and they looked back down at the Book and continued to read.

And remembered all the Books that came before…

About the Author

Jamieson is a Number One Best Selling Author. But he didn't used to be. He thinks that is totally awesome and likes to mention it to anyone. Sometimes even those unfortunates at the bus stop. The less said about that, the better.

For longer than he has written novels or novellas of the romantic nature, Jamieson was a short story writer. He returns to his roots in this collection, away from the soft flicker of firelight and into something darker.

It's nice to let the creative side out to play every now and again, right?

You can learn more about Jamieson at
www.jamiesonwolf.com

www.ingramcontent.com/pod-product-compliance
Lightning Source LLC
Chambersburg PA
CBHW060616130626
46555CB00002B/531